GW01459214

TIME TO DIE

A HARRY BAUER THRILLER

BLAKE BANNER

RIGHTHOUSE

PRAISE FOR HARRY BAUER

"Thor, Baldacci, Flynn, Hamburg. Get ready as Banner fits right in!"

AMAZON REVIEW

"Move over Jack Reacher there's a new guy taking over."

AMAZON REVIEW

"Great stuff. Exciting and fast paced. On par with Flynn & Thor."

AMAZON REVIEW

"The writing was superior, the story line was compelling and the action was top-notch. Sorry I could only give this one a five star rating!"

AMAZON REVIEW

Copyright © 2025 by Right House

All rights reserved.

The characters and events portrayed in this ebook are fictitious. Any similarity to real persons, living or dead, is coincidental and not intended by the author.

No part of this book may be reproduced in any form or by any electronic or mechanical means, including information storage and retrieval systems, without written permission from the author, except for the use of brief quotations in a book review.

ISBN-13: 978-1-63696-434-8

ISBN-10: 1-63696-434-6

Cover design by: Damonza

Printed in the United States of America

www.righthouse.com

www.instagram.com/righthousebooks

www.facebook.com/righthousebooks

twitter.com/righthousebooks

Do not go gentle into that good night,
Old age should burn and rave at close of day;
Rage, rage against the dying of the light.

Dylan Thomas, Do Not Go Gentle into That Good Night

ONE

Is death black or white?

Is it a folding of light into darkness?

From where I sat on my deck, I could see a pristine blanket of virgin snow clean across the plain to the Wind River Mountains, maybe ten miles distant. They rose spectral into a clear blue sky, more like the ghosts of mountains than solid rock, shimmering out of frozen, white death.

The air was cold, like ice. The woodcutting axe lay across my lap, and I held the whetstone in my left hand. I don't know how long the thought lasted, but when I reached for the demitasse of black coffee beside me, it too was cold. Cold and black, a different kind of death.

I took the bottle of Bushmills and added a dose of whiskey, drained the cup, and set to sharpening the blade of the axe with long, slow, rasping strokes. I was going to need plenty of wood for the fire.

A distant movement caught my eye. A quarter of a mile away, the track from my cabin met the thin, black line of Pole Creek Road. Down there, I could make out a big, black RAM nosing in past the mailboxes before starting its slow, lurching climb through the snow. I could have cleared the path after the snowfall, but I hadn't wanted to. After laying Miriam to rest up in the mountains, after setting her soul free among the peaks[1], I had sought isolation. Leaving two feet of snow on the track had helped with that isolation. Now the approaching truck gave me a bad feeling. Somebody was about to intrude on my isolation, and I thought I knew who that was.

I got to my feet. Unconsciously I left the whetstone on the table beside me but kept the axe loose in my right hand as I followed the decking around toward the parking area at the back of the cabin, keeping my eye on the Dodge all the while. It crunched to a halt outside my kitchen door, the door opened, and I was surprised to see Colonel Jane Harrison climb out. She had swapped her usual blue business suit for Levis and boots and a large, red quilted jacket. We stood a moment frowning at each other. Her cheeks were red, and there were clouds of condensation issuing

---

1. See *Harry Bauer 21, The Cell*

from her mouth. She nodded at the axe in my hand and said, "This is a true Harry Bauer welcome. You going to hit me with that?"

I tried not to smile. "I guess that depends on why you're here. You want a coffee?"

"It beats getting hit with an axe."

She pulled an attaché case from the back seat and followed me into the kitchen, where she left her case on the breakfast bar and moved into the living-cum-dining area. There she stood looking around. I had several large logs burning in the fireplace, the room was warm, and there was an agreeable aroma from the wood smoke. The light from outside was dimmed slightly by the snow that had accumulated in the corners of the windows.

"This is beautiful," she said. "It's very homey."

She sounded like it surprised her. I glanced at the clock on the wall. It was nine-thirty a.m.

"Did you have breakfast?"

She turned to look at me and smiled. "Yes. I had something on the plane." I put her cup of coffee on the breakfast bar and showed her the bottle of Bushmills. She gave her head a small shake. "The coffee is fine."

She removed her quilted jacket. I pointed to the living room area, which was sunk a couple of steps below the dining area and the kitchen. We carried our coffee over and sat beside the fire. I found myself returning her smile, surprised that I was pleased to see her.

"I think it's the first time I've ever seen you in anything but your blue business suit. The jeans, the sweatshirt..." I gestured at her with an open hand. "It's nice. But I notice you brought your attaché case, so I'm guessing this is not a social visit."

A cloud passed over her smile, and she gave her head a small, sideways twitch.

"Well, Buddy was going to come himself."

Buddy was Brigadier Alex 'Buddy' Byrd, the overall director of Cobra, the unofficial agency I sometimes worked for.

The colonel gave a small frown. "I think you know, Harry, that for a long time, the brigadier has dealt with you personally, even though I am the director of operations. Because..."

She trailed off and shrugged. I gave a small laugh.

"Because you and I were always at each other's throats."

"Yeah, because of that, among other things. But I haven't seen you for a while, Harry, and I never really thanked you properly for everything you did for me when I was abducted by Gabriel Yushbaev..."[2]

She trailed off again.

I nodded once slowly and gazed at the dancing orange flames in the fire.

---

2. See *Harry Bauer 8, Breath of Hell*.

"Not many people can render me speechless, Jane, but this would not be the first time you've managed it." I turned my eyes on her and waited till she met my gaze. When she did, I told her, "Thanks. Thanks for coming yourself, and thanks for telling me why you did."

"As a team, we seem to be pretty good at blowing things up. Let's see how we make out building a bridge together."

"You got it."

"Do you hear from Beverly at all?"[3]

"She sends me a card occasionally. Her dad is less communicative."

"Must be hard for him. He wasn't able to rescue his daughter, but you were."

I raised my shoulders an eighth of an inch. "Must be. I guess." Then I couldn't help adding, "I was thinking of her, not him."

We had that awkward moment where two people who like each other realize they have nothing to talk about. She drew breath a couple of times, then put down her cup and said, "Perhaps I should tell you about the job, and you can tell me if you are willing to take it."

"Sure." We both stood to go and get her case; she laughed, I smiled. "I'll get it, sit and get warm by the fire."

I got the case from the breakfast bar, brought it to the

---

3. See *Harry Bauer 21, The Cell*

living room area, and handed it over. She watched me do it, smiling. As she took it, she said, "This is the other Harry, huh? I've only ever known you in your..."

She hesitated. I laughed as I sat. "In what Marvel would call my other identity? I guess Stan Lee would have called me The Grim Reaper."

"Maybe so. I didn't expect this." She indicated the cabin. "I guess I expected a gym, weights, several sacks, protein drinks, and pizza."

There was a ghost of mischief in her face.

"That's all downstairs. Except the pizza. What's the job?"

She nodded and snapped the catches on the case.

"Did you ever hear of the Sisak killings?"

I frowned at the ice crystals making prisms of the light on the window. "Kind of rings a bell. Sisak is in Croatia, right?"

"Between July 1991 and June 1992, during the Croatian War of Independence, members of the Croatian Army and the Croatian Sisak Police Department illegally detained, tortured, and murdered a large number civilians from the city of Sisak. The victims were Croatian Serbs. The detentions, murder, and torture were part of a program of ethnic cleansing, the objective being to encourage the Serbs to leave Croatia."

I set down my coffee and ran my fingers through my hair. "This was the breakup of what used to be Yugoslavia, right? When the Cold War ended, Tito died, and what had been Yugoslavia broke up into Slovenia, Croatia, Bosnia Herzegovina, Serbia, Montenegro, Kosovo, and Macedonia."

She nodded, then took a deep breath. "Really, from February or March 1990 to March 1991, tensions were building throughout what was still at that time technically Yugoslavia. Tensions were at their highest in Croatia, which had a very large Serbian minority. There were political moves in Croatia to introduce democratic elections, and in April, the first elections were won by the Croatian Democratic Union, which supported separation and independence. But there was real fear among Serbians that this party would institute a pogrom of Serbs. To complicate matters, the Serb Democratic Party won majorities in a number of Croatian towns including Korenica, Kim, and Benkovac. Ethnic tensions increased, and there was not only a powerful move on the part of Croatia to secede from Yugoslavia but also among towns with Serbian majorities within Croatia to remain under Serbian control. So not surprisingly, by March '91, Croatia was sliding toward all-out war. The Republic of Serb Krajina declared it was seceding from Croatia to join the Republic of Serbia, and the Government of the Republic of Croatia declared their intention of a rebellion. In June 1991, Croatia declared its independence from Yugoslavia, and full-scale war erupted. It lasted until 1995."

"So far this is nothing new."

"Stay with me. I am setting the scene. Sisak is a city in central Croatia, about thirty-five miles south of Zagreb, the capital. It had at that time a population of about eighty-five thousand people, of whom about fifty-five thousand, over half, were Croats, and less than twenty thousand—less than a quarter—were Serbs.

"By 1991, Croatian Serbs in Sisak and the surrounding areas began to suffer threats of violence, and soon after that, there began to be abductions, killings, and what became known as disappearances. Precise figures are not available, but it is estimated that as many as twenty-one Serb villagers were massacred on August twenty-second alone that year, when Croatian forces conducted house-to-house searches in a number of villages, seeking Serbian paramilitaries who had fired mortars at Sisak.

"Another twelve at least were reported to have been executed in March the next year. A lot of the victims were tortured before they were killed. This included breaking arms and legs, stabbings, and decapitations. In addition to those known cases, another sixty-five bodies were exhumed and found to have been tortured and murdered. An unknown number, running possibly into hundreds, vanished without a trace."

I drew breath to ask a question, but she plowed on.

"In 2012, Vladimir Milankovic and Drago Bosnjak, two high-ranking members of the Sisak Police Department, were put on trial for war crimes. Milankovic was found guilty and convicted, but Bosnjak was acquitted. The fact is that after the war, the atrocities committed by the Serbs were seen to be so extreme, and public opinion was so strongly against them that there was little stomach at the official level to bring any kind of case against Croatian officials, much less to conduct the kind of investigations that would make them stick.

"So in the end, a large number of officers and officials who had ordered or committed crimes against Serbians, including the torture and massacre of civilians, not only went free but were rewarded and promoted to positions of power and influence."

"And I am guessing it's one of those people I am going after."

"Yes. His name back then was Bogdan Novac. Born November 8th, 1955, which puts him in his mid to late thirties in the early '90s. He was a sergeant in the Sisak Police Department but is known to have headed up a paramilitary group known as the Hawks. We know he and the Hawks were responsible for massacres in at least three villages near the border with Bosnia Herzegovina, but there was one in particular which we were able to get compelling evidence for and which was particularly grotesque."

She reached in her attaché case and pulled out a large manila envelope which she handed across to me.

"Here are the details with the evidence we were able to accumulate. You can study it in detail later. In general terms, the Sisak Police Department suspected that there was a Serbian paramilitary group based in the village of Babina Planina. So the Hawks were dispatched there in a number of Land Rovers and four armored cars equipped with heavy machine guns. Estimates vary, but we figure there must have been between thirty and fifty heavily armed men.

"They rounded up the villagers, possibly over a thousand people all told, herded them into the town square, and began systematically to murder the children one by one in front of their parents and families. As you can imagine, the mothers broke down pretty soon and gave Novac and his men the information they wanted."

"Who the members of the paramilitary group were and where they were based?"

"Precisely. But once they had that information—pretty soon, after they had sacrificed three or four kids—instead of releasing the hostage villagers, Bogdan Novac ordered the wholesale execution of the entire village. Their bodies were hung from lampposts, and many of them showed signs of having been tortured and maimed prior to death as a warning to others. Their actions were indiscriminate, and the victims included men and women in their eighties, mothers, fathers, and their children, many of them Serbo-Croat mixed marriages. It was horrific."

"This guy was never arrested or processed?"

"No. He was promoted, became a senior member of the police, and took early retirement in 2015 at the age of forty-nine. Curiously enough, that coincided with Amnesty International delivering a file to the International Court of Human Rights requesting that he be investigated for crimes against humanity."

"Didn't they investigate?"

She shook her head. "They couldn't. A fire at City Hall in Sisak destroyed a whole swath of official records including birth certificates, death certificates, employment records, passport and ID cards—you name it. They included all the official records relating to the life and times of Bogdan Novac, and at the same time, all computer records relating to him were also mysteriously wiped. Suddenly, overnight, Bogdan Novac ceased, officially, to exist."

She pulled another envelope from her case and handed it over. "However, some investigation carried out independently has produced some results, and it looks as though Novac might have changed his identity. At the Babina Planina massacre, Novac and a number of the other men involved stole a great deal of money and property. It seems Novac then got involved in gun running and drug trafficking and amassed a small fortune. We are talking about several million dollars, and it looks as though he may have used that to acquire a new identity and reinvent himself in Norway."

I screwed up my forehead and stared at her. "*Norway? Why Norway?*"

She gave a one-sided smile. "You probably just answered your own question, Harry. If you're hunting someone who has stolen ten or twenty million dollars and is trying to disappear, you're more likely to search for them in Bermuda, the Bahamas, Brazil, or Panama than you are in Norway, right?"

I nodded. "Right. Yeah, I guess so. You have twenty million dollars in the bank you'll be looking for sun, sand, and a life of luxury."

She gave a small laugh. "So if you want to avoid being seen or recognized, you're a damned sight better off in a place like Norway, where there is minimal tourism and a very small population. What are there, five and a half million people in the whole country? That's less than a third of the population of greater Los Angeles, and most of them are concentrated in three or four cities, including Oslo, which has something like a quarter of the population of the whole country." She gave a small shrug. "A smart guy trying to disappear might well move to a place like Norway or Wyoming, right?"

I nodded for a bit, then shrugged. I had to admit she had a point.

TWO

I TOOK SOME TIME TO GO THROUGH THE material she had given me. First I looked at the details of the massacre at Babina Planina, and then the other massacres that were also attributed to Bogdan Novac. Though no concrete proof existed, the weight of evidence made it almost indisputable that it had been the work of the Hawks, and that he was leading them. The details were horrific, and as always, it was the most vulnerable who had suffered the most—the very old, the very young, and the weak.

When I had studied and assimilated the details of the crimes he had committed, I studied the evidence that Bogdan Novac was now Dante Gallo, an Italian originally from the small town of Trieste, right on the border with Slovenia and a mere fifteen miles from Croatia. If it was him, he had made a smart trade-off: where the proximity to Croatia risked linking him with the place, it also provided a reasonable explanation for any physical or linguistic peculiarities belonging to that area. I knew that in Trieste they spoke a peculiar dialect which they called Triestine, which included a mix of Venetian, Italian, German, and Slovene, as well as Greek and Serbo-Croat.

As an Italian, he would have freedom of movement within the European Union, and as a native of Trieste, nobody would question his imperfect Italian or English, or whatever language he was using.

The evidence, though it was mainly anecdotal, was compelling and did include a certain amount of photographic evidence. Curiously enough, the anecdotal evidence was more persuasive than the photographic, which was based on a comparison of photographs taken twenty or twenty-five years apart. A man's face can change a lot between the ages of twenty-five and fifty.

Dante Gallo now lived on the island of Odinnsey, off the north Atlantic coast of Norway, in a small town called Asketreby, about fifty-five miles west of Trondheim, two hundred and eighty miles northwest of Oslo. It was what you'd call remote.

It seemed he had a small shipping company in Trondheim, on the fjord. The company was called Sokol Shipping. I did my due diligence, and Google informed me, via my cell phone, that Sokol in Croat meant hawk. If this guy was Novac, the name of his company revealed a reckless, arrogant side to his personality which was in contrast to the cautious intelligence that had taken him to a very remote part of Scandinavia instead of Marbella or Puerto Banus or Brazil.

While I studied the file, the colonel sat quietly and watched the fire. When I was done, I put the material on the table beside me and studied her face for a moment. I was distracted briefly by the deep orange and amber light on her cheeks and her brow until she blinked and turned to look at me.

"I'll do the job," I told her. "But I need to be a little more sure that he is our guy. It looks like he is, but I need to be certain before I execute him."

"I agree, and that was the brigadier's view too. He almost didn't accept the contract. It was borderline, but he decided that what evidence there was suggesting it's him is compelling enough, if you will agree to confirm it as part of the job."

I thought about it, looking out at the white gleam of the snow under the sun.

"Go there, to Norway, to Odinnsey, make contact..." I trailed off, and she finished it for me.

"See if you are satisfied. If you feel there is any kind of reasonable doubt, abort. If you're sure, execute the mission."

I took a deep breath and nodded. "OK, I'll do it.

Obviously I won't be going as me. You have some documents?"

"Of course. You'll be going as Clark Kent. We even have some glasses for you."

"Funny."

She handed me a final envelope. I emptied the contents onto the table beside me. There was a passport, a couple of credit cards, and a driver's license.

"You are Borg Nielsen, an American of Norwegian descent. You teach Norse mythology at the University of Colorado Boulder. It's an online course."

"Slow down." I blended a smile and a laugh. "I know Thor was the god of thunder and agriculture and he was a bit stupid. I know Odin was the god of war, had one eye, and hung upside down from Yggdrasil to learn the meaning of the runes. That's about it."

"You know more than I do then. I suggest you visit Amazon and acquire the book *Bullshit Your Way in Norse Mythology*."

"Thanks."

"Nobody is going to engage you in conversation about the Viking gods, Harry. It's just a name and an excuse for being in Norway. If anybody checks, UCB will confirm they have a Professor Borg Nielson. You're in Norway researching a book you are writing."

"What kind of book? This is hard stuff to bluff."

"Any book you like, Harry. It could be a textbook, a

Viking murder mystery, or a Scandinavian thriller. Your choice. And it's easy to bluff. Just say you don't want to discuss it until it's finished and published."

I grunted. "I didn't realize you were so devious."

"Really? How do you think I made colonel in a man's world? Just try to use a four-syllable word occasionally instead of a four letter one." She suppressed a grin and added, "Get Buddy to give you a list."

"Boy, we are on form today, huh? Thanks for the advice. What about weapons?"

She sighed and smiled at the same time. "Harry, don't get mad, OK? You're the best. I know you're the best. We all know you're the best. But *please* don't blow anything up. This needs to be a clean, low-key job. It's one of a few jobs jointly commissioned by Central Intelligence, the British Secret Intelligence Service, and the European Union's Military Intelligence Unit—as well as, unofficially, the Norwegian Ministry of Defense. They have all stressed that they expect the job to be done discreetly. If you can make it look like an accident, you get brownie points."

"Understood. Again, what about weapons?"

"We have a case specially adapted. It will take your Sig Sauer, two loaded magazines, and your Fairbairn and Sykes concealed in special compartments. I have it in the RAM. There will be no C4, no RPGs."

"I get it, Jane."

"You'll fly to Oslo and get a connecting flight to Ørland Flystasjon on the Trondheim Fjord. From there, you will get the ferry to Asketreby on the island of Odinnsey. We called the hotel there, Sigrid's Gjestgaard, and asked about booking a room. They said just turn up. It's first come first served, but they always have rooms. Once you're there, get chatty. You know how to be chatty?"

"No, but one of me has multiple personality disorder, and I'm pretty sure one of them is chatty."

She studied me and gave her head a small shake. "You are a strange man, Harry Bauer. So get chatty about the local area, the Viking gods, any standing stones in the area, folklore—"

"I get the idea, Jane."

"OK, but let it be known you are on a sabbatical and plan to hang around for a long time. Maybe ask about renting a cabin or something. Buddy thinks that will deepen your cover."

"Right."

"You'll also be provided with something pretty neat the tech department has come up with. It's a set of photographic projections based on facial recognition software which will give you a pretty good idea of what he must look like now—"

"Unless he's had plastic surgery."

"Correct, unless he's had plastic surgery. The

Company is making discrete inquiries. We don't hold out much hope. A *lot* of people have had plastic surgery in Europe in the last ten years, plus there is nothing to stop him from going to Brazil to get it done there."

"Right. Or Thailand."

She gave a brief nod and went on. "The tech department has also developed a set of photographs using the same software showing more clearly what he must have looked like around the time he disappeared."

"How old was he then?"

"In his late thirties or early forties. Also, I can't promise anything at this stage, but we're trying to get a sample of his DNA plus details of any birthmarks, scars, moles, and any other peculiarities he may have had."

I frowned. "How are you going to manage that?"

"His doctor, Dr. Josip Harvat. He's come forward because he claims to have disapproved of what the Hawks were doing. We'll see. I'll keep you posted on that."

I nodded a couple of times. "OK, so move in, establish my cover as Borg Nielsen, an academic on sabbatical, identify Bogdan Novac, eliminate him, ideally make it look like an accident, and move out..."

"Yes." She went quiet and shifted her gaze to the fire. I watched her a while, then let my gaze drift to the motionless white fields outside. After a while, I said, "There's something else. What is it?"

"We've been here before, Harry, and you were not happy about it."

"Where is here, and what was I not happy about?"

"A couple of your recent operations have hurt some very powerful people."

"People?"

"Yes, people. Let me explain this, and please listen without getting on your high horse. These are just facts, OK? Not my opinion."

"I'm listening."

"We are hearing chatter from Moscow, from Tehran, from China—even from the EU and the Five Eyes. You have been noticed, and a growing number of agencies want to know who you are and above all who you work for. It's not just official agencies, either. The Russian Mafia, the Mexican Cartels, and..." She hesitated a moment and narrowed her eyes at me. "What is more worrying, Harry, is that extremely powerful people within the infamous military-industrial complex that Eisenhower worried so much about have also become aware of you and want to know who you are, who you work for, and whether you are a threat." She lifted her shoulders and let them drop. "It's not just that you have made some pretty noisy hits. It's also the nature of the victims. These people are beginning to notice a pattern."

"There's not a lot I can do about that. I can't take

somebody out just because they suspect I exist. That's exactly the kind of stuff we don't do."

She gave a small laugh that declined into a sigh. "No, they're not people we can take out. The CIA is our biggest concern because of its close ties to the military-industrial complex, but there are others like MI6. Agencies that can expose us and make our activities public. That would finish us, and we could all spend the rest of our lives behind bars, or worse."

"Like you said, we've been here before. The brigadier has connections. Why can't he just pull strings and get them to back off?"

"No." She gave a couple short shakes of the head. "Think it through. With the Pentagon or MI6, we might be able to pull strings short-term, but it would just confirm the fact that we exist and stoke the interest we are trying to kill. Also, then you have to ask what about the Russian Federal Security Service, the SVR and GRU? What about the Iranian MOIS? And you know yourself that Sinaloa wields a budget these days comparable to many countries and has been known to cooperate both with enemies of the United States *and* the CIA."

"I understand, Jane, but I am not sure what your point is. You want me to stop blowing things up. I have said I'll do that. They want Novac's death to look like an accident. OK, I'll do that too." I raised my shoulders. "What else?"

"You're under active surveillance."

"Who by?"

"The Agency and the Iranian Ministry of Intelligence and Security. Those two we know for a cert. But there may be private interests involved too. You really upset Iran with the Beverly Cook affair[1]. You may have upset some private interests too."

I shook my head and gave a small, humorless laugh. "Again, either you want me to do the job or you don't. You just gave me the job and now you're saying we need to abort? Which is it?"

"No, Harry. That's not what I am saying."

I frowned. "Well, what then?"

She stared me straight in the eye. "You need to be retired."

I stood and walked to the window. Death still lay cold and white across the plains.

"Jane, we have discussed this in the past. I went through a bad patch, but I am back, and I am not ready to retire."

I turned to face her. She was watching me from her chair in the shadows. "Hear me out, Harry. It's not that simple. If you are caught and tortured, however tough you are, we both know there is a breaking point for everyone. That puts the whole agency at risk."

---

1. See *Harry Bauer 21, The Cell*

"We all assumed that risk when we joined."

"Yes, that's true. But surely it's something you need to think about. Would you really bring the agency down and see Buddy in prison? I don't think you would. But there's more to it than that even. You have changed as a person since you joined. Back when you started, you were a loner, and you shunned people. But since then, you have made connections. There's Buddy and me for a start, and other people too. There is Dr. Claire Erickson right here in Pinedale. And there is Beverly Cook, whom you just rescued. These people all matter to you, and because of that, they are ways to get at you. I hate saying this, Harry, but it is a fact, and you know it, and we have to address it."

"Am I going crazy? You came here to offer me a job and at the same time tell me I need to retire?"

She took a deep breath. "What I am saying is it's something that has to be addressed. You are Cobra's best operative, but you are also becoming its biggest liability. There are too many ways for hostile agents to get to you, and if they do get to you, they get to Cobra. We have to address that."

"So you are telling me I have to retire..."

"Can you think of any other way of neutralizing the risk?"

I returned to my chair and sat. "Does the brigadier agree with you?"

"He suggested it. And I suggested I should come and discuss it with you."

"Why? We don't have a great track record of easy understanding and great communication."

"For that very reason. It's a habit we should break. Whether it comes from me or from him, it's the same set of facts, and it's the same problem. It has to be addressed and solved. I have a suggestion, and I want you to listen to it very carefully."

"What is it?"

She shook her head. "Not here. I want you to come back with me to DC for a meeting with Buddy, General Nathan Tetley, and the Director of Intelligence Networks. We may be able to use this job to achieve our ends. But we discuss it in an hermetically sealed office, and only we five know the details. Are you willing?"

I nodded. "Of course. When do you want to go?"

She looked at me for too long before answering. When she did, her voice was a husky whisper.

"Tomorrow," she said. "Early tomorrow morning."

"You'll stay over?"

"If..." She hesitated. "If you'll have me."

I smiled on the right side of my face. "A dying man's last wish. I'll have you."

THREE

WE TOUCHED DOWN AT RONALD REAGAN National Airport at noon and were met on the tarmac by a Range Rover with official agency plates, tinted glass in the rear windows, and a driver and his mate who would have made King Kong think twice. They had the obligatory blue suits stretched over their pectorals and biceps, the obligatory wire in their ears, and the standard Secret Service issue aviator sunglasses. It was hard to tell them apart, and I wondered idly as I opened the door for the colonel whether they were cloned at Area 51.

I climbed in after the colonel and slammed the door, and we took off at speed, moving north past Arlington National Cemetery. We followed the Potomac along the George Washington Memorial Parkway at an easy ninety miles an hour. On our left, the woodlands grew steadily denser as we progressed, and the river began to fall away on our right. Pretty soon, we hit the Fort Marcy interchange, and it was as we approached the overpass ahead that we saw the lights on the far side flashing red and blue. The driver began to slow, and his pal pulled his badge from his inside pocket and lowered the window.

There were two patrol cars parked at the side of the road on the grass with four cops watching the cars, slowing them down and mostly waving them on. As we approached, one of the cops stepped onto the blacktop and raised his right hand to us, pointing to the grass shoulder with his left. The colonel sat forward.

"What's this? Drive on."

"I don't know, ma'am."

He flashed his lights at the cop but only managed to make the cop's gestures more aggressive as he stood directly in front of us, legs straddled and right hand ordering us to halt. A second cop had come out behind him, waving the traffic into the inside lane. We slowed to a crawl, and the guy in the passenger seat leaned out of his window holding up his badge and shouting, "*Get out of the way, will you! Look at the goddamn plates!*"

There were now three cops blocking the way and shouting at us to pull over, pointing at the shoulder. The driver stopped the car but didn't pull over. He lowered his window and leaned out. On the right, his pal was having a shouting match with one of the uniforms. I could hear the cop yelling, "*If I tell you to pull over, I don't care who the hell you are, you pull over!*" But I was watching the sergeant who was approaching the driver.

I was watching him because he was unfastening his holster as he was walking. The driver was saying, "Are you out of you goddamn mind?"

"I am ordering you to pull over onto the grass, sir!"

"Will you look at the plates, please? We are Secret Service, and we have government officials—"

"I don't care who the hell you are! Pull over onto the grass. I won't tell you again!"

"I'm going to reach in for my badge—"

As he said it, the colonel leaned forward and said, "Pull over, Ash," and simultaneously the cop yelled, "*Do not reach in your jacket!*" and his weapon was in his hands. The driver and his pal raised their hands. The sergeant shouted, "*Pull over onto the grass. Now!*"

The colonel said, "Do as he says, Ash. I'll talk to them."

Ash put on his right indicator and eased slowly onto the grass.

Of the four cops, one stayed on the blacktop waving the traffic past. The other three came over to the Range Rover. The sergeant still had his weapon in his hand.

"Get out of the car!"

Ash looked at him and spoke quietly. "Are you out of your mind, Sergeant?"

The sergeant pointed at him with his left hand. "I am not going to tell you again, sir. Get *out* of the car! Now!"

The colonel sighed. "This is ridiculous." She leaned forward and spoke to the cop. "Sergeant, I am Colonel Jane Harrison of the Central Intelligence Service. I am going to get out of the vehicle to talk to you." To me, she muttered, "Stay where you are." To Ash and his pal, she said, "You too. Stay where you are."

She opened the door and stepped out. The sergeant had raised his gun and took a step back. "Ma'am, get back in the car."

She raised her voice. "I am Colonel Jane Harrison of the Central Intelligence Agency. You have seen our plates, and you have seen my drivers' Secret Service badges. If you want to keep your damned job, you are going to *get out of our way! Sergeant!*"

He still had his gun trained on her. "Get back in the car, ma'am."

"Brigadier Alex Byrd, General Nathan Tetley, and the Director of National Intelligence are waiting for us at an urgent meeting. What is the *matter* with you?"

"Get back in the car, ma'am."

I had drawn breath to tell her to get back in, but she snapped, "I am going to get my phone—"

The sergeant yelled, "*Do not reach in your jacket!*"

I watched her hand go inside. I reached for the car door. I saw his weapon spit fire and jump. I saw the shell circling slowly in the air. Hours seemed to pass as I reached for the door. I saw the individual beads of blood glisten in the sun as they erupted from her chest. I heard shouts of rage and astonishment. I heard two shots like firecrackers. Then I saw the sergeant's gun explode again as the colonel dropped to her knees.

Then the door was open, and I was falling out onto the grass, reaching for her where she lay in a pool of blood. I could hear my own voice yelling, "*Jane! Jane!*"

I saw her eyes were open and unseeing and knew that meant she was dead. I looked up into the eyes of the sergeant. In my peripheral vision, I could see the other three running for their cars. I met his stare. He was aiming directly at my chest, and I knew it was over. This was how it ended. The weapon exploded. I felt a stab of pain in my chest, and blackness closed in.

And as consciousness faded, a voice in my head told me, "Death is black."

———

LIGHT HURT MY EYES. I had them closed, but there was a glow filtering through my eyelids. Somewhere in my mind, I was thinking that if I was dead, it shouldn't hurt. But when I heard myself groan, I was pretty sure dead people didn't groan, so I opened my eyes and shielded them with my hand. I went to sit up, and somebody drove an iron spike through my head. I swore profusely and with feeling. The pain eased, and I made it to a sitting position.

I was on a sage green sofa. To my right, there was a large, marble fireplace where orange flames were glowing and wavering in the semi-dark. That made me realize the lights were off and evening was closing in.

I looked to my right and saw there was a tall window beside the fireplace, and outside I could see large trees under a dusk sky. I stood and felt momentarily nauseous. The room swayed but then settled. Ahead of me, there was a white door. There were a couple of sage green armchairs and some dark wood bookcases. Over on my left, I saw a sideboard, and on it, there was a range of bottles and decanters and some glasses. I spotted a bottle of Bushmills, crossed the room on unsteady feet, and poured myself a generous measure. After the second pull, I felt better.

I was groggy, but in my mind, I started to go over what had happened: the lights, the cops telling us to pull over. The official plates with the department clearly displayed. The cops pulling their weapons with no provocation. On an official car. That doesn't happen.

In DC, that doesn't happen.

I drained the glass and made for the door with a hot coal in my gut. I wasn't all that surprised to find it unlocked. I opened it and stepped out into a broad, not very long corridor. At the end, it opened out into a wide hallway with a large door, a coat stand, and a very large vase of dried flowers. To my right, I could see a set of walnut doors which stood open onto what I guessed was a drawing room or a library. From within, I could hear the murmur of voices. One I recognized as the brigadier's. The other was the colonel's. Apparently I wasn't the only one who had survived being shot in the heart.

I walked to the doors and stepped through. It was a large, comfortable library with four tall French windows that showed a very green, wet lawn and an Italian garden. Here there was also a fire burning in a marble fireplace. Beside the French windows, not far from the fire, the brigadier and the colonel were seated in a couple of burgundy chesterfields at a heavy, round table. She had a gin and tonic; he was drinking a martini. I leaned on the jamb. The brigadier saw me and stopped talking. The colonel turned to look at me.

I said, "I guess I just got retired."

The brigadier spoke with no expression on his face. "I'm afraid so, Harry. I apologize, but we had no option. There were lives at risk. Not just ours, but innocent civilians, and a child."

"It's the third time. Third time lucky, huh?"

"Come and sit down. How are you feeling?"

I paused a moment to look at the floor. It looked like a genuine Persian carpet.

"You mean aside from mad enough to tear that marble fireplace out of the wall and shove it up—"

"That'll do, Harry. I understand you are angry. I would be too, in your place. Anyone would. But let's keep a clear head. Come and sit down and have a drink. Whiskey?"

I gave it a second, nodded, and crossed to the table. While the brigadier filled my glass, I stared at the colonel. She avoided my eye.

He spoke over his shoulder. "If it is any consolation, Jane was in fact opposed to the plan. She was working strictly under my instructions."

I raised an eyebrow at the colonel. "Strictly under your instructions, sir?"

There was an edge to my voice. She got it, her cheeks flushed, and her eyes flooded with angry tears.

The brigadier said, "Yes, and if you'll leave the fireplace where it is, I would like to explain to you exactly what the situation is."

I didn't answer. The colonel stood as the brigadier put my glass in front of me.

"Excuse me a moment, Buddy," she said. "I'll be right back."

She hurried from the room, and we both sat staring at the doors as she passed through them and closed them. He looked at me, and I said, very quietly, "Just exactly what were the instructions you gave her, sir?"

I turned to look at him, and his face was like stone.

"To bring you here and set up your assassination along the way. I gather something personal has happened between you two. That is none of my business, just so long as it doesn't interfere with our work. But I hope, Harry, that after all the years we have worked together, you know me well enough to know there are lines I will not cross."

I didn't answer right away. Eventually, I nodded. "Yeah, I know that."

The colonel returned five minutes later with a face like a summons. Her eyes and nose had that look like she'd just had a bad coughing fit. She sat in her chair and looked me in the eye.

"As the brigadier has indicated, a lot of careful thought was given to the matter. For the record, as the brigadier has already said, I was opposed to the assassination plan. In particular the fact that you were not to know about it. We are all painfully aware of your independence and your stated desire to live as yourself according to your own lights. On those grounds, I opposed it."

I said, "Thank you" quietly to my thumbs.

"However, as the brigadier—"

"Buddy. You always call him Buddy. I call him sir and the brigadier. You call him Buddy."

She sighed through her nose. "As *Buddy* pointed out, we are a military unit, and sometimes we just have to take orders. Whoever we are. The situation as it was put the unit at risk and, what was more unacceptable, it put civilian lives at risk. You will object that we should have informed you—"

I shook my head. "We discussed this once before, and I was intransigent. You knew I'd react the same way."

She frowned like two and two weren't making four the way they were supposed to. "In any case, after discussing it, the brigadier ordered me to go and give you a basic briefing and, if you were willing to take the job, to bring you to DC for a full briefing. That was the full extent of my orders."

I held her eye. "I understand."

She ignored me and went on. "The hit was very realistic. A fleet of ambulances and police officers showed up almost immediately and cleared the scene. It was filmed, and we have reviewed the video in detail. News of the hit, with names listed, will be in all the papers and on network news by this evening. So you are officially dead."

The brigadier nodded once and said, "I'm sorry, Harry."

"I guess being officially dead beats being actually dead."

"That is a positive reframe."

"However." It was the colonel again. "We cannot guarantee one hundred percent that you won't be traced or followed to Norway. There are departments of Central Intelligence who are very interested in you and in the possibility of an assassination agency such as Cobra. After all, it is part of their brief to make friends with some of the people we exist to eliminate.

"Tehran is also very keen to get hold of you and interrogate you. If we are lucky—and very careful—we might be able to persuade them, and others, that Harry Bauer is now dead, and so is the organization that used him. We will do our best. We need you to do the same."

"I'll do my best."

She put her attaché case on her lap and opened it, then took out a large manila envelope. She tossed it on my lap.

"Forget Borg Nielsen. He died with Harry Bauer, just in case your house was bugged or was being surveilled. Look at the contents and familiarize yourself with them. You are Saul Goldman, from a conservative upper middle class New York family. You trained as a commercial lawyer and became a partner in a Manhattan firm, Black and Chase, but after your wife's death in a car accident, you had an epiphany and decided to do something meaningful with your life. Now you are looking for a place to write your first novel."

I nodded. "OK, good, it has all the virtues of the previous cover, but it is more low-key and believable."

She listened like she wanted to slap my face, then went

on. "You have your documents and credit cards in there, plus a detailed background. Please study it and memorize it. If you identify any issues, please let the brigadier know. Have you any questions?"

"No."

"Good. Then I suggest you familiarize yourself with Saul Goldman and pack a couple of suitcases. Your plane departs tomorrow evening." She turned to the brigadier. "Is there anything else, Buddy?"

He shook his head and said quietly, "No, thank you, Jane."

"I'll be going then."

She stood and made for the door. As she opened it, I said, "Colonel, there is one thing." I turned to the brigadier, and he sighed and looked away. I said, "Excuse me one moment, sir."

I rose, followed her out into the hall, and closed the door behind me.

"Jane, I'm sorry. There is no excuse. I apologize unreservedly."

She nodded once. "Yes, Harry, you're right. There is no excuse. What you implied was unforgivable and deeply insulting. It's too late. I have had enough. Go to hell."

She turned and walked away. I watched her leave, then went back and joined the brigadier in front of the fire. He said, "Is it resolved?"

"Yeah."

"This cannot happen again."

"I understand."

"Good. Then let's get this job done."

FOUR

I WATCHED MYSELF GET ASSASSINATED NEXT DAY on various news channels on the plane. It wasn't as bad as I had expected, but watching the colonel getting shot was still hard, even though I knew she was alive because she had told me to go to hell just a few hours earlier. In the first broadcasts, it had said that the identity of the victims was not known, though they were known to be driving in an official vehicle, but later editions identified the colonel by name and rank, the two Secret Service agents, and Sergeant Harry Bauer, late of the British SAS. No known next of kin.

They had done a good job. It must have been hard to pull off without leaks. I was sure the brigadier had hauled on some pretty heavy strings and called in a few favors. I had suspected for a long time—and this display went a long way toward convincing me I was right—that Brigadier Buddy Byrd had a pretty comprehensive database of incriminating evidence on a wide range of people around the world. He wasn't the kind of man to abuse it, but it was there for when he needed it.

Of course, it was true that the Five Eyes top brass—the guys who carried real weight at the Pentagon, the Whitehouse, Whitehall, Wellington Street, the Lodge or Premier House—were all confident that they had the brigadier secured with very little wiggle room. They had, if nothing else, his guarantee of absolute plausible deniability, and they could throw him to the wolves in Congress or the International Court of Human Rights any day they chose to. But they also knew damned well that the brigadier was no fool and would never take control of an agency like Cobra without covering his back and taking out serious insurance. At the very least, they knew they would be spending the rest of their lives looking over their shoulders, waiting for that tap on the door at four a.m.

But what the colonel had said was true. However well they'd pulled it off, there were sure to be men in blue suits and dark glasses at my funeral, watching the coffin as it was lowered into the sod and asking who had I worked for? Who had killed me? And what had I done that had led to this elaborate execution?

It crossed my mind that it would have been good to discuss it with the colonel, but I had blown that possibility. And maybe this time, I had blown it for good. Even I had to recognize I had crossed a line by a good, long stretch.

After that, I ordered myself a whiskey to toast myself an uneventful flight over Bifröst to Asgard and Valhalla and settled down to sleep.

We touched down at Oslo Lufthaven International Airport on schedule at nine in the morning. I waited for the other passengers to get off before me. Though I was pretty sure I had not been tailed, if I had, this would be a good chance to spot it. But nobody struck me as suspicious or out of place. You develop a sixth sense for that person who doesn't belong. It's in the way they walk, the way they move, and the way they look around. It's all too casual. There was no one there like that. They all belonged.

Once the last few passengers were shuffling out, I squeezed into the aisle, pulled my bag from the locker, and made my way into the tube that led to the terminal. Passport control and baggage reclaim were uneventful, and I went to the A gates in the west wing to get my connecting flight to Ørland Flystasjon for another half hour's flight into the mountains and the fjords.

That also was uneventful, and a Scandinavian breakfast of crusty bread, pumpernickel ham, and cheese with plenty of coffee got all twelve of us to Hårberg, where the small airport of Ørland Flystasjon was located in little more than an hour. There was no tunnel there. We climbed down the steps and crossed the tarmac on foot under a cool, late morning sun. The landscape all around was very flat and very green. There were blue and orange clapboard houses dotted here and there with gabled roofs, and all in all, it reminded me of North Dakota.

I found a taxi cab at a rank out front, where all the cabs seemed to be Volvos. The driver had that kind of tranquility you develop sitting around fires telling stories about crazy gods while you wait for the snow to melt sometime in the next six months. He had the kind of moustache you might grow during those months, just to pass the time, too, and pale blue eyes that found the rest of humanity a bit amusing.

Before I could speak, he took my cases and slung them in the trunk and said, "*Uthaug Ferja* goink to *Asketreby a Odinnsey, har jeg rett*? Am I correct?"

It didn't sound like anything I had ever heard, so I smiled and showed him on the map what I wanted. He rumbled like he thought I was funny but didn't want to offend me and opened the rear passenger door for me to get in.

Uthaug was a small collection of clapboard houses

with gable roofs, chimneys, and white picket fences, of the sort you would not be surprised to find anywhere from New England to Washington State. There was a harbor where the water was so cold it looked creamy and seemed to move more slowly than normal water. There was a ferry that looked a lot like a large fishing boat that had been adapted by an enterprising owner to accommodate people instead of fish, and there was a small clapboard café with a handful of Formica tables inside and a couple of wooden benches outside.

We pulled up outside the café. The giant with the moustache made a slow, contemplative job of pulling my cases from the trunk, told me the fare while he pointed at his meter so's I'd understand, and then pointed at the café, grinning among his moustache.

"Ticket, tee-ket, *ferja* go *Asketreby a Odinnsey, har jeg rett*? Yo? Yo!"

He winked at me, climbed in his cab, and left. I still have no idea what he said to me.

In the small café, I bought a ferry ticket and a cup of coffee. There was no room in the café, so I carried them outside and sat at a bench.

Around me, the benches started filling up. Some of the people had no luggage at all but carried that air of belonging there. They had come over for the day and were now returning home. Others had rucksacks, and those tended to speak with Australian or American accents.

They were there because they had seen the *Lord of the Rings* movie and the Marvel movies about Thor and wanted a taste of Nordic magic.

But there was one guy in his sixties with a head that was bald on top, though he had a long, white ponytail drawn back from just above his ears. He had a deep scar on his left cheek that made him look ironic. I saw him talking to the guy I assumed was the captain of the ferry. They were loading an old Toyota truck onto the deck, which was in turn loaded with sacks, boxes, and crates of what looked like food and drink, including everything from potatoes and salad to meat, wine, and beer.

When he was done, as if driven by some kind of collective telepathic intuition, people started grabbing their things and making for the gangway. A tall lean blond kid at the foot of the gangway took their tickets as they boarded. I drained my coffee and followed them. I stowed my luggage and found a bench out on the prow. There I sat and gazed out at the stretch of cold, dark ocean, surrounded by the brooding mountains and the scattered islands.

The diesel began to rumble, and the old wooden boat began to vibrate. Pretty soon, the mooring lines were being cast off, and we were easing out into the fjord, thudding slowly out toward the Sea of Norway and the Island of Odinnsey.

We were just a few minutes out, and the air coming off

the icy water was making me shudder, but it's not often you get to sail across a fjord in late autumn, so I thought I'd stick it out as long as I could.

Behind me, I heard the door open and slam. I looked around and saw the guy with the ponytail doing a balancing act toward me. He nodded.

"You look like an American," he said.

"You sound like one. Midwest?"

He sat opposite me and handed me a beer. "You nailed it. Jan Olafsen. Haven't been home for a few decades." He took a swig and nodded back toward the cabin. "I seen you had a couple of suitcases. Don't see a lot of suitcases around here. Rucksacks, shopping bags, or trucks like mine stocking up on provisions. Don't see a lot of suitcases, though."

I smiled like I was a bit embarrassed.

"Saul, Saul Goldman." I held out my hand, and we shook. "Thanks for the beer. I am probably a walking cliché. I just jacked in my law practice in New York and came here to write my novel. I guess you get a lot of people doing that."

He chuckled and nodded. "Sure do. I did it. So you're definitely not alone."

I shrugged. "Life's too short. You gotta carpe the diem before the reaper carpes you."

"That's a writer talking, right there."

I gave a smile of ironic uncertainty. "What about your novel? Did you write it?"

"Nah." He shook his head, looked at the sea for a bit, and then raised an eyebrow at me. "Real writers can look at the ugly shit and express it in words. Other people, people who are only playing at being writers, they express the ugly shit in silence. We clam up and don't want to talk about it."

I nodded. "I get that." I tried to look like a man conflicted about admitting his pain and said, "I lost my wife not so long ago. Part of why I'm here."

He studied my face a moment and grunted.

"I was in the Marines, Marine Force Special Operations Command. I saw a lot of stuff, did a lot of stuff." He took a swig and gave a chortle. "See, right there? I'm calling it stuff and being as vague as I can be. A writer wouldn't do that. A writer would use some elegant well-turned phrase that would take you there, right there where they had been."

"Huh." I made a face and nodded. "That's an interesting insight."

"It's not mine. I can't claim it. So I opened a bar and a small hotel instead, in the remotest part of one of the most remote places in Europe. I figure people who go on vacation to remote places are going to be interesting, right?"

"I guess so. That makes sense. Not that I'm interesting, but I am looking for a place to stay. You got a room for me?"

He raised his shoulders. "There are only two places on the island. There's the Ravnereiret, up near Koloya Bay." He shook his head. "You don't wanna go there. And then there's my place. I run the bar. My daughter runs the hotel. We can ask her when we get there. She refuses to book rooms. She says people book and then cancel and she ends up losing money. The upside is if you turn up out of the blue, chances are she'll have a room for you. The place is clean. She has high standards, like you'd expect from a Marine's daughter. The food is good, and my bar is right next door."

It was twenty-one nautical miles to Odinnsey. Our cruising speed seemed to be about 10 knots. That put the crossing at somewhere in the region of two and a half hours. Something told me I had struck a gold mine with this guy. He was sociable, willing to talk, and ran one of the few bars on the island. I was about to ask him about the non-Norwegians on the island when he piped up with, "So, Saul, any idea yet what your novel is about?"

"My wife told me a long time ago I should write about the Jewish Experience, but I told her back then, I'm like Joseph Heller. He said he had no idea what the Jewish Experience was. He was just a New Yorker. I'm thinking, you know, I come from one of the most densely populated places on the planet. What I'd like to write about is a small, remote island where everyone has lots of space, they are isolated from the world and from each other, and how that brings out their private, inner secrets." He grunted softly, so I went on. "And it doesn't only have to be the Norwegian fishermen. I'm ready to bet there is a colony of interesting foreigners here too."

Just the corner of his mouth was smiling. His eyes were inspecting my face. It went on for a few seconds that became almost uncomfortable. The only sounds were the splitting, foaming water at the prow and the occasional cry of a seagull overhead.

"Yeah," he said finally. "There's what you might call a small community of foreigners. Mainly we are outcasts and refugees from that other reality. The one you're escaping from."

Was there a hint of irony in the way he said it?

I smiled and averted my eyes. "Am I detecting something in your voice?"

He watched me take a pull on my beer. When I set down the bottle, he said, "You're not a lawyer."

I arched an eyebrow at him. "I'm not?"

"You're military."

It is not often I find myself unable to respond to a situation. But looking at the guy's eyes, we both knew. If you're in special forces long enough, you develop a kind of sixth sense. I could smell it off him just like he could smell it off me. When that happens, the best thing you can do is recognize it.

I gave a reluctant smile. "You can't hide it, can you?"

"Nope."

"British Special Air Service. But you're wrong about one thing. There is nothing to stop an ex-operative becoming a lawyer."

"Right." He said it without much conviction. "Just tell me something. Are you coming to our island as an operative or as a lawyer who wants to reinvent himself as a writer?"

"I guess that's me. I'm not here to cause trouble, Jan. I'm just here to try and deal with my ghosts."

He nodded for a while, regarding my face. Then he smiled. "If that's true, Saul, you are welcome to Odin's Island."

"Is that what Odinnsey means?"

"Ey is island. So yeah, literally Odin's Island. There is a legend that the tree, Yggdrasil, where he hung upside down and lost his eye so he could get the secret of the runes, was on this island. The town, Asketreby, translates as Ash Tree Town. Yggdrasil, the tree that contains the three worlds, is an ash tree, and as the legend has it, it was right here, in our town on our island."

I smiled and decided I liked this guy. "That's pretty cool."

"It's cool." He got to his feet, a little unsteady against

the growing swell. "Catch me when we dock. I'll give you a ride to my daughter's hotel."

"You got it. Thanks."

I watched him go inside, then sat staring at the ocean, enclosed by its ring of mountains and islands, and wondered if Jan Olafsen was going to be a help or a problem. Something told me all he gave a damn about was his daughter, but you never can tell.

FIVE

WE EASED WITH DESULTORY BURSTS OF DIESEL
into the port. The port was two long, concrete quays that
had been built out into a cove, making use of small, scattered islands as support. The old ferry eased in, between
the arms of the quays, and drifted toward the mooring
blocks at the far end. Truck tires had been hung along the
hull and the side of the piers, and they squeaked loudly as
we drew up against them. Next thing, there were guys
leaping ashore and mooring the boat to large, iron
bollards.

A ramp was set up, and Jan's truck and one other were
driven down to the quay. There I approached him among
the bustle and leaned on the open window.

"Your offer still stand?"

"Sure, climb aboard. It's a little over a mile northeast

of here, as the crow flies." I climbed in and slammed the door. He went on. "Asketreby is a small town. There might be a hundred inhabitants all told." He glanced at me and smiled as he fired up the truck and pulled away. "That rises to maybe a hundred and twelve during the holiday season. I hope you're going to find enough material to justify two suitcases."

To say the landscape was bleak would be an understatement. Norway is green and lush, but these North Atlantic islands were dark gray rock with parched, withered yellow grass poking through, ravaged by icy winds. Through this blasted landscape we moved along something that was not so much a road as a track with a thin layer of disintegrating asphalt spread over it. It was rough and rutted, and we rattled along at little more than ten or fifteen miles an hour. Even so, it was less than ten minutes before a cluster of clapboard houses painted bright reds and yellows and purples began to appear, rising out of the parched, yellowed ground.

There were no terraced cafés, restaurants, or anything like that. There was nothing you could really call a street or a road, except the one we had arrived on, which continued out west and a little north. It was just a scattering of low, colorful gabled buildings. The closest thing to a central point was a small, wooden church. A short distance from that was the only two-story building. It was double-fronted, with two rows of windows on either side of the door and a sign that said *Sigrid's Gjestgaard* across the upper floor.

He pointed with his wrist on the steering wheel. "That's my girl right there, Sigrid. My bar's opposite."

He pointed to a place maybe fifty feet across a dusty, beaten area. You wouldn't immediately guess it was a bar. It was almost indistinguishable from the houses, but there was a small, illuminated sign in one of the windows that said *Bar.*

He gave a chuckle. "We don't advertise much. There's not much point. There are a couple of shops and a mechanic. He takes care of the plumbing and electric too, but you wouldn't know unless somebody told you. They all look just like houses. Anyhow, if you're staying with Sigrid, you won't need shops. She'll take care of you."

He pulled up outside the burgundy building with white window frames and helped pull my cases from the back. Then he slapped me on the shoulder before he climbed back behind the wheel.

"Maybe I'll see you tonight."

"You might at that."

I picked up my cases, opened the door with my elbow, and pushed inside. The place was empty. The floors were pine, the walls were pine, the ceiling was pine, and there was a broad pine staircase to the upper floors. On my left, there was a pine desk with an old Bakelite telephone on it. Behind it there was a half-open pine door. On my right, there was a large stone fireplace burning large chunks of pine and a huddle of three calico sofas and four armchairs all in different, cheerful colors. It was warm, and there was an agreeable smell of pine resin in the air.

I left my cases by the nearest sofa and went to the counter. There was a brass bell, and I gave it a smack with the heel of my hand.

She leaned out the half open door, chewing. She gave a 'my mouth's full' smile, and the rest of her followed out to reception. She was holding a large bread roll stuffed with cheese and ham in her left hand and pointed to her mouth with her right. It was cute. I smiled.

"I'm in no hurry," I told her, "and swallowing food whole is advisable only if you are a boa constrictor or an ostrich."

She narrowed her eyes, smiled some more, chewed, and swallowed.

"You came with my dad."

"I did?"

"The guy in the red Toyota."

"I did. I can't say there's a family resemblance." She was shorter, maybe five-six, with very black hair, though her eyes were a dark blue.

"Yeah, I take after my mom."

"I'm glad. Have you got a room for me? Something large and comfortable. I don't know how long I'll be here. Your dad told me I don't want to go to Ravnereiret."

There was no computer. She opened a large, red ledger and bit into her sandwich again. "No, you don't wanna do that." And then, "A writer, huh?"

I frowned. "Wow, is it that common?"

She gave her head a small shake. "No, my dad called me on his cell." She glanced at me and suppressed a grin. "It's a beef he has because he did it, and everything he wrote was crap." She slid the ledger over for me to sign. "He's telling you his story like it's the most unimportant thing that never happened. Who wants to read that, right? You have to write like you give a damn about what happened."

She turned her back on me and pulled a key from a pine pigeonhole in the wall. She handed it over and told me, "It's the closest thing we have to a suite. There is no terrace, but the window overlooks Asketreby Avenue and has sweeping ocean views."

"Is there a bellboy I can tip for carrying my cases?"

"Nope. Up the stairs and first on your right. We do have a dining room, however, and I am told the food is good, if you like whale blubber and seal meat."

"It beats what I ate in the Colombian Amazon."

She gave me the narrowed-eyes smile again. "I was joking. We're all about salmon, island goat, and ox."

"No vegetarian or vegan?"

"Yeah, if we catch one, we roast it as a special on Fridays."

I carried my cases up to my room, which was large and spacious and had a comfortable lounge with an open log fire. It was burning well, and I figured Dad must have called her from the ferry.

I unpacked, showered, and stretched out on the bed for a couple of hours. Norwegians have their dinner about four or five in the afternoon. So at just before five, I dressed and went downstairs, where I found I was the only person in a small dining room with half a dozen tables and a window that looked out on rocky desolation that managed somehow to be beautiful.

The tables were set with white linen, and the glasses sparkled. The kitchen door bumped open, and Jan's daughter came out tying on a long, black apron.

"Anywhere you like," she said. "You're alone."

I sat by the window and debated making a wisecrack about what my mother had said to me when she kicked me out aged four. Instead I said, "You're Sigrid, right?"

"Why?" It wasn't hostile, just blunt.

"Because Jan Olafsen's daughter is too much of a mouthful."

She hitched her shoulders. "Jansdota has three syllables. Elizabeth has four."

"OK, I'll be staying here for a while, you're cute, and I'd like to know your name."

"Oh, OK. Yuh, Sigrid is my name. That's why the hotel is called Sigrid's Gjestgaard."

"You got a smoked salmon salad?"

"I can make one for you. I have also a roasted leg of island goat. You should have that. It's real good. Don't have wine. We have no good wine. But the ale is fantastic. I make it myself."

She didn't wait for an answer. She gave me a smile and a wink and walked back into the kitchen. When she came out again ten minutes later, she had a big tray with a bowl of salad, a basket of hot, crusty whole-wheat rolls, a stone jug, and two pint-sized steins. She set it all on the table and sat opposite me.

"I will eat with you," she said. "It's lonely and boring in the kitchen. Tell me if you like the salmon. I smoked it myself, and the sauce is from English mustard and honey."

I broke a roll and tasted the salad. It was good, and I made noises that said so. She said, "Why are you here?"

"I thought your dad told you when he told you to prepare the suite for me. I'm writing a novel, remember?"

"I think that's a lie," she said in that same direct Scandinavian way it is so hard to take offense at. I frowned and chewed at her. She said, "I think you have some other reasons."

"Yeah? What makes you think that?"

"My father told you he was in the Marines?" I nodded as I chewed. "He was in special operations. Ho probably told you this as well."

"He did."

"I remember his friends, when I was small. My mother left when I was just very young, and it was my father who raised me. He raised me like I was one of the troop. And those men, his friends, they had a..." She looked around the room, rubbing her index and middle finger against her thumb, like she was feeling something and looking for it on the walls and the ceiling at the same time. "A quality, a feeling about them."

"Yeah?" I gave a small shrug that asked what that had to do with me. "Must have been an interesting childhood."

She stabbed a piece of salmon and shoved it in her mouth, then pointed at me with her fork. "There are lines most people don't cross. Society has conditioned us so deeply that crossing those lines causes extreme anxiety. The kind of man I am talking about has crossed the most important of those lines. He has given himself permission to cross that line. He has killed another human being, and still he has found some kind of peace."

I had finished the salad. I wiped my mouth with a napkin and sighed. "Why are you telling me all this?"

"Because you are one of those men."

"You are saying I have given myself permission to kill other human beings? You have deduced that in the time it took me to eat a salad?"

She nodded. "I can see it in your eyes."

I sighed again, deeper. These are the things you just

can't foresee. This is why your cover story needs to be very carefully chosen.

"I was in the Army," I told her. "We saw action. When the other guy is trying to kill you, you already have permission from your government to take him out. But in that moment, you're right, you have to give yourself permission to kill him. Afterwards, when the adrenaline ebbs out of your blood, you need to make peace with what you've done."

She was watching me, nodding, calibrating what I was saying. I knew then I was going to have to be careful with her. She was much more of a risk than her dad. Him I could handle. She was an unknown quantity.

I said, "I'm not in the Army anymore. I am here, on this remote place, because I want to process all that by writing my novel. It might be a crap novel, I don't know. But right now, I am writing it for me. That, and that alone, is the reason I am here."

She smiled. It was a nice smile. "That," she said, "and my roasted goat."

"That is the other reason."

She got up and went to get the goat from the oven. It was still sizzling when it reached the table. To say it was exquisite would be almost an insult. The skin was crisp and wafer thin, and the meat was succulent and tender and full of subtle flavors.

"Wood oven," she said with her mouth full, so it sounded like "Boomf obbeng."

We devoured it, and as we were cleaning the bones like a couple of cavemen, she said, "OK, buy me a drink at my dad's bar, and I can show you the characters for your book."

"Sounds like a plan. Everyone goes there?"

She stood, collecting the plates. "Pretty much. Either there or the Ravnereiret. But it's a different clientele. There's nowhere else."

"I kind of assumed most foreigners here would be recluses and hermits."

Her glance was direct to the point of being unnerving.

"There are a couple of recluses. Is that what you're looking for? A recluse? A hermit?"

"Don't tell me," I said and laughed. "You have all of Agatha Christie's books, and you have a passion for reading crime novels."

"No," she said as she backed through the kitchen door with her hands full. "I read people."

SIX

THE PLACE WAS SURPRISINGLY CROWDED AND noisy. The music was some kind of stream which mixed everything from 1960 to the mid-eighties, with plenty of Scandinavian heavy rock thrown in. There was a big, open fire in the right-hand wall as we came in and an iron stove as backup against the far wall. The bar was on our left, and Jan was behind it with a guy who looked like a younger version of him, only he had a beard big and bushy enough to be a nature reserve.

She pointed to a table near the fire. "Grab it. I'll bring beer and a couple of chasers."

I went and sat and was grateful for the warmth of the flames. The strange sing-song of the babble was agreeable to the ears, too. She returned pretty soon with a couple of tankards, a bottle of Johnny Walker, and a couple of shot glasses. As she sat, I decided to go right in.

"So who are the interesting foreigners here?"

"Norwegians are not interesting enough for you?"

I took a pull on my beer and smiled as I set it down. "Native populations in remote places tend to be pretty tame. It's the people who come from outside who bring secrets. Like your dad said, they are usually running or hiding from something."

She knocked back her whisky, smacked her lips, and took a pull on her beer.

"This is not Colombia or Mexico, or the Caribbean. It's not even the Costa del Sol in Spain. They get a lot of shady characters there escaping from the law. But..." She paused, staring at her tankard for a moment, then shrugged. "But also, it's not quite as quiet and tame as you might think." She leaned back. "You know, there are settlements on many of these little islands. There is not a lot of money to be made here. We have the Draugen oil field, but it employs few people, mainly graduates from the mainland. So—" She gave another small shrug. "Maybe you'd be surprised at some of the things local people do to supplement their income."

"Yeah? Surprise me."

"OK, let me give you some interesting facts. The Draugen field is just fifty miles from us, northwest. From there, it's four hundred and sixty miles to the Faroe

Islands. That's about four days in a decent yacht. From there, it is a couple of days to the United Kingdom, or almost the same distance to Iceland. And then you have a long haul, one and a half thousand miles to Newfoundland with a possible stopover in Greenland. That's ten days, maybe two weeks. Do you know what we call this?"

"No. What do you call it?"

"The secret corridor. You know why?"

"You keep asking negative rhetorical questions. No, why do you call it that?"

"Because all the shit that comes up from Thailand, Afghanistan, and Turkey goes through Russia to St. Petersburg, Belarus, and Kaliningrad, or Poland, and then goes from *there* across the Baltic into Scandinavia. Everybody is so fixated on Mexico and the Gulf of Mexico—now the Gulf of America—they forget that Afghanistan and Turkey and the Golden Triangle of Myanmar, Laos, and Thailand produce more than ninety percent of the world's illegal opium and a lot of heroin. So if you have all that heroin and opium, what do you do? Send it across the Pacific? Or do you ship it through a corridor of the most corrupt police forces on the planet and slip it into Europe and USA via the secret corridor?"

I smiled. It was an incredulous smile because I thought she was bullshitting me. "Wow, you've done your homework. But what are you telling me, that half the world's opium and heroin trade comes through Odinnsey?"

She didn't look amused. "I didn't say that. I said that we were in the secret corridor. This little archipelago off the coast of Norway makes a great place for yachts and boats to set off for the UK or for America on the route I described. The narcotics departments of Europe and the USA are focused south and east, and in the States, it's all Mexico, Mexico, Mexico. But there is a stream through Russia and Belarus and Poland—and not just drugs; there is slave and sex trafficking too—that goes across Scandinavia and into Canada, and they just ignore it. It must generate tens of billions every year. That stream does not attract cops, but it attracts other kinds of people. People like Hells Angels. You won't see them much here, but you will see them at the Ravnereiret. Now I have a question for you."

I was becoming interested. I said, "OK."

"Are you telling me that you are not here because of that secret corridor?"

"No, I am not telling you that. I am not telling you I'm not, either. What I am telling you is that I am here to write a novel. Why is that so hard to believe?"

She stared at me for a long moment, then flapped her hand at me. "Nah, ignore me. I'm a Scorpio. My dad is a Scorpio too. We are always suspicious of everything and trying to uncover mysteries where there are none."

I shrugged. "Beats playing Candycrush on your cell phone all day. But now you've got me curious. Do you know of actual people who are into this trade? You mentioned Hells Angels. I don't see any. Or is it all kind of conspiracy theory?" I spread my hands. "It could be a good basis for a plot. Maybe you're helping me here."

She shook her head. "It's not just a conspiracy theory, Saul. A couple of people who got too curious have disappeared and then been found washed up on the beaches. You don't last long if you get dumped in this water. You die of a combination of accelerated hypothermia and drowning. It's not a nice way to go. We had an investigative journalist here a couple of years back. He was researching climate change, but he got talking to me and my dad, and we told him about the secret corridor, and he decided he was going to investigate that too. He disappeared. We figured he'd gone back to Paris or wherever it was he'd come from." She shook her head. "But he showed up at Little Bogøya Bay, in the sand. He was all puffed up and blue." She shrugged. "People who ask too many questions get washed up on beaches, all blue and puffy."

"OK, so I shouldn't ask too many questions of the wrong people. But I can ask you questions, right? And what I can't get through asking you questions, I can make up. That's what writing is all about, after all."

She drained her beer and refilled our shots.

"You shouldn't take it as a joke. The cops won't touch

it; I don't know why. It can be really upsetting, you know? Your friend gets washed up on the beach, and you know the man who killed him. Maybe he comes into your bar for a drink, or into your restaurant, and you have to serve him, and when he pays you, he touches you with the same hands he used to drown your friend."

I knocked back the shot and picked up my beer while I swirled whisky around my mouth. I swallowed and said, "You lost a friend" before draining the beer.

"Yeah, I lost a friend, in pure, civilized, twenty-first century Scandinavia. A friend who was a little too curious, thought it was all a gas and a bit of fun. Same story. He disappeared and was hooked a few days later in a fishing net."

"I'm sorry."

"Hey, nobody gets out alive, right? It's not about *if* you go, it's about *how* you go." She pointed at me. "Your round." She held out her hand. "Give me the money. I'll go get 'em. It'll be quicker."

I gave her twenty kroner and watched her push her way through the crowd toward the bar. The one over-riding thought in my head as I watched her was, what the hell were she and her dad trying to tell me? And inextricably bound up with that question was, how the hell did they know they had to tell me anything? My instinct was to dismiss what Jan had told me about one special ops guy recognizing another as bullshit. Which would mean they had some other way of knowing who I was and that I *was due to arrive.*

But that was even less probable, and the fact was, what he had said was true. It's like they nail a sign to your forehead that says, *Fuck off, I'm Special Ops.*

I didn't have long to mull it over. The man himself appeared a moment later carrying a tray. There were three beers on it. He set it down, then he set his ass down on one of the chairs and distributed the beers.

"I can't stop long. Sigrid is minding the bar. She's been telling you about the shit that goes down here, huh?"

"More like the shit that goes through."

"Right." He thought about it a moment, then said, "Some goes through, some goes down."

"She seems to think I am here because of that. You both do."

"Yeah?" He took a pull on his beer and set it on the table carefully. "Well, Saul, I ain't gonna pry. You're more than capable of knowing what you're doing. What I ain't so clear about is whether you know what goes on up here."

"No, I have no idea. It's what I keep telling you. One of the reasons I'm here, Jan, is because I know nothing about the place. It's remote and desolate." I gave a small, humorless laugh. "But from what Sigrid and you keep telling me, maybe I hit the jackpot! Maybe I've come to a gold mine of literary convertible stuff!"

"I'm going to tell you what happened to Olaf. Olaf was a fisherman. He had a small trawler and a few men who went fishing with him. They all made a good living, and they were good friends. But Olaf was a bit wild, you know? A bit crazy. So on a few nights, him and his men saw yachts coming and going, and they had a pretty good idea what it was about. It was contraband, smuggling, and you didn't need to be Sherlock Holms to know what they were trafficking, right?"

I gave a nod. "Heroin and opium from the southeast through a Russian corridor."

"Sure, and you might think, that happens everywhere, so what's the big deal? The big deal is that in New York or London, or LA, you have millions of people living their normal, suburban lives and big police departments to keep things in check. Here you have a few hundred people living in a confined space with no police department."

"There are no cops on the island?"

"There's a police station on Sørburøy, the main island, three miles away by boat. On a stormy night, you might as well be in the middle of the Atlantic. And even if they responded, they have one sergeant and one constable. Unarmed. You see"—he glanced around with an ironic smile on his face—"officially we have a zero crime rate. Why? Because nothing ever gets reported. Anything that goes down is either dealt with locally, or people are too scared to get involved."

I took a pull on my own beer. "So Olaf was the exception. He got involved."

"He did that. He had two daughters and a wife, and he didn't like the fact that drugs were passing through his island. He was old school and big enough to get away with it. He came in here one night, and the crew of one of those yachts was here."

"A local?"

"No, I think he's Russian. Boris Petrov. Big guy, crew cut, bad eyes, man. Cruel eyes. He comes in to the bar with his crew sometimes. He's taken an interest in Sigrid. He has a house out at Kunna Point. Big place with a natural harbor. Keeps a couple of yachts there."

"So he was here that night."

"Yeah, and Olaf says to him, 'I see your boats taking shit over to the Faroes.' So Boris begins to laugh, and he tells Olaf, 'It wasn't to the Faroes. It was to the Orkneys. And you and your family are better off not knowing that.' So Olaf, instead of keeping his mouth shut, starts getting wild. And Olaf wild is a dangerous guy. He says to Boris, 'You mention my family again, and I'll cut out your tongue and shove it up your ass, pig's penis.'"

"Pig's penis?"

"Yeah, it's what they say around here. So now—" He shrugged and spread his hands, expressing the inevitable.

I said, "So now Boris has to kill him."

"Right? There was a fight. Boris had a crew of five,

and they tried to hold Olaf. Olaf broke one guy's jaw and another guy's arm. He knocked a third guy unconscious with a hammer blow to his head. And I was beginning to think he was actually going to cut Boris' tongue out. But Boris ain't stupid. He can see how things are going, so he pulls a gun on him. His two remaining crewmen grab Olaf, and Boris just sticks a knife in his belly and pretty much disembowels him right there."

I sighed. It was a depressingly familiar scenario. "Nobody did anything."

"He had a gun. Seventeen rounds. How many people would he have killed before anybody subdued him? And every one of us, Olaf included, knew that behind him there was the Russian Mafia. So yeah, somebody did something. Boris took his injured men and Olaf's body, and we went and got a bucket of hot water and bleach."

"This Boris lives on the island?"

"Yeah, some of the time. But stay away from him and his operation. He is dangerous. I mean seriously dangerous."

"So he runs the island?"

He made a face. "Almost."

"A rival gang?"

"Some guy over on the western side of the island, at Koloya Bay. He bought the Ravnereiret. It's like an old-fashioned inn. He bought it and then built himself a big house on the bay. They say he has a shipping firm in

Trondheim or some shit. I know he has a small army at his house and some very bad people running the inn. And I know the Mafia and the authorities leave him alone."

"Yeah?" I laughed. "It sure looks like I came to the right place to write my book. What's this guy's name?"

He shook his head. "I don't know, and I don't wanna know. I'm tellin' you all this so you won't go digging. These people mean business, Saul. I don't wanna see you get killed the way Olaf was."

I smiled. "Don't worry, Jan. I don't want that either, and I appreciate your telling me. I know you could have looked the other way just as easy. Thanks."

"Tell me you're going to take this serious."

"You know enough about me, Jan, to know I will take this seriously."

He smiled and nodded. "I've worked with the British SAS. I know enough about them to know that when a blade says he's going to take something seriously, half the time it means he's going to kill everyone involved."

I laughed out loud. I had a vision of a sergeant I'd known, a big New Zealand guy we called the Kiwi, eyeballing me and saying, "We have got to take this seriously," and that was exactly what he'd meant. He meant we had to wipe out a whole camp. You really don't want to be taken seriously by the SAS.

I gave my head a shake. "I told you, Jan, and I don't know how else to tell you. I'm here to write a book. I don't want to complicate things. I just want to write my book."

He smiled and raised his glass to drain it. It was his way of saying he didn't believe me, but he'd done his best. Now it was up to me.

He was right about that. It looked like I was going to have to take the situation very seriously indeed.

SEVEN

Across the room, I could see Sigrid watching us as she served drinks at the bar. Jan stood and paused, leaning his hands on the back of the chair.

"There's one more thing," he said. "Don't get me wrong, but are you thinking of getting involved with..." He hesitated. "With, uh, with my daughter?"

I let my eyebrows crawl up my forehead in genuine surprise. "What the hell are you talking about, Jan? Involved how? I'm staying at her hotel. That's it. I only met her a couple of hours ago."

"You know what I mean, Saul. I mean, are you attracted to her?"

"Sexually?"

His face flushed. "Don't use that word when you're talking about my daughter!"

I was frowning and shook my head, not in denial but in disbelief. "Hell, Jan. She's cute, but no. It hadn't even crossed my mind. Also, she's got her dad right across the road and what is more to the point, she has shown absolutely no sign of being interested in me. So no."

He nodded and said to his hands on the back of the chair, "Small, remote communities. Things get intense sometimes."

"Right." I nodded. "I can see that. But Jan? I am going to tell you one last time. I'm here to write my novel. You are giving me plenty of material. It's been what, four or five hours, and I've been accused of being a CIA spy, military intelligence, DEA, a hired killer, and wanting to hit the sack with your daughter. I think that's enough for one day. Can we relax now?"

He laughed quietly and walked away. Sigrid crossed him on her way back. She sat and pulled her beer over.

"He gave you his talk?"

"He did. He's pretty intense. And he refuses to believe I just want to be quiet and write my book."

"He told you about Olaf?"

"He did that."

"I wasn't here. I was across the road. But he told me about it. It scared him. He's a tough guy, and he's no chicken. But that scared him."

"I'm not surprised. This Boris guy sounds like a psycho."

She glanced unconsciously at the door. "You'll probably get to meet him one of these days. He comes in quite often."

Her words, what her father had said, the dark, claustrophobic environment, it suddenly made sense. I leaned back in my chair.

"He has a thing for you. He wants you to be his girlfriend." She turned to stare at me, and I made an intuitive leap. "It's worse. He's given you a deadline."

Her eyes went wide. "How could you possibly know that?"

"Two and two, they invariably wind up making four. All your dad's warnings, and yours, and then he asks me if I am into you. It all adds up to, 'Sigrid is Boris' property.' Am I mistaken?"

She sighed and closed her eyes. "He's been coming on to me." She opened them and shrugged. "I think it turns him on that I am the only person who has ever said no to him."

"Men like Boris don't take no for an answer."

"No, they don't. And he hasn't."

"So either you already gave in to him, or he gave you a deadline to make up your mind."

"He gave me a week. I have five days left. Either I am his Odinnsey girl or he will burn down the bar and the hotel."

"Son of a bitch. Have you informed the cops?"

"Of course not. If the cops get involved, he will kill my father and then rape and kill me."

"So what are you going to do?"

"I don't know. Dad says I should refuse, and he will take care of them. But that's crazy talk. I've been refusing to think about it, like if I ignore it hard enough it will just go away. But in the end"—she raised her shoulders a fraction of an inch—"I just don't have any realistic choices..."

"Can't you both leave the island?"

"It's not that easy. All of Dad's money is invested here. If we ran, we would have nothing. We are not entitled to social benefits in Norway because we're American citizens and..." She hesitated and spread her hands. "Dad can't go back to the States. Don't ask."

"And your dad plans to take on Boris' gang single-handed?"

"He wants to negotiate with him, appeal to his better nature. Some shit like that."

There was a brief lull in the music. A gust of wind howled at the door. I said, "How do you think Boris will react to that?"

She wasn't looking at me. She said woodenly, "Why don't you ask him yourself?"

I followed her gaze. There were six of them. Five of them were dressed in the unofficial uniform of the ex-special ops guy. The Levis, the brown leather jacket, the heavy boots good for kicking, and the real short hair. The sixth one was an anachronism. He knew it, and he culti-vated it. He was a good six three, powerfully built, and he had that same Russian special forces look about him. His head was like a lump of rock, and his hair was more like a coating of coarse sandpaper. But his double-breasted suit was a very dark blue raw silk. It looked like something from one of those Italian designers with more artistic passion than taste. It wasn't so much cut as draped, like a tailored toga. His shirt was light blue, and his tie was yellow. Maybe he'd poked his tailor in the eye before he made the suit.

He moved through the bar greeting people, and they all seemed to take a sudden interest in their shoes. He called to Jan behind the bar, ordering drinks for his boys. His destination was clear. He arrived at our table and gave Sigrid the kind of smile that curdles fresh milk. Then gazed at me.

"I look for you at hotel," he said, and shifted his gaze back to Sigrid. "But they tell me you have come to Papa's bar with a man."

She spread her hands. "What's your point?"

He looked at me again. "Who is your friend?"

She sighed. "Boris, this is Saul Goldman, a guest at the hotel."

He stared at me for a long moment. "Saul," he said at last, like he wanted to remember my name when he killed me. "Goldman. A Jew."

I smiled. "Like Karl Marx," I said. "And Boris makes you East European at the very least, perhaps even Russian. I haven't the benefit of your surname. Will you join us?"

He came around the table and sat with his arm draped across the back of Sigrid's chair. It was a gesture of possession, or property owned.

"I am wondering," he said, "what brings an American Jew to an island like Odinnsey."

I smiled broadly and pointed at him like my finger was a gun. "That is a real coincidence, Boris. Because I was asking myself, what brings a Russian draped in blue silk to an island like Odinnsey? So we were both asking the same question about each other. Ain't that something?"

"You don't answer my question?"

"Oh, I didn't realize it was a real question. Because mine, you see, was not a real question. I am here to write a novel."

"Novel..."

"Yeah, a novel. And I need somewhere peaceful and tranquil where people will let me get on with my work. Because you see, Boris, the book is about the eight years I was with the British SAS, and I killed a lot of people and did some really bad shit in that time. So I need peaceful relaxation to be able to write about it."

He smiled a genuine smile for the first time. "You, an American Jew, was in British SAS?"

"For eight years."

"So you have killed, and people have tried kill you. You have lived this experience."

I shrugged. "It was a job. You get the job done, and you go home."

He turned to Sigrid, who was looking away at one of the small windows. He pointed at me. "You see this. Bloody American Jew was in SAS. They try to kill him. He kills many of them. Is he crying? Is he telling stories, 'Oh! I was so brave'? Hell no. This American Jew, he say, 'It was job. I do job. No big deal. Just a job.' This is guy with balls. Big balls."

"Yeah? Like you?"

He ignored her and leaned across the table toward me. "I was in special forces too, in Russia. People try to kill me. I killed many. Nobody know what this feel like. Only people who have lived this can understand. Is like secret brotherhood. Am I right?"

Sigrid groaned and raised her eyes to heaven. He didn't notice, and I tried not to smile.

"Listen good to what I am saying. There is a brotherhood all over the world among those guys in special forces—I don't care the country or the race or the fuckin' religion. Even among enemies. Men like you, a fucking American Jew, and me, a fucking Russian son of a bitch. We have been to the edge of life, and we have looked over in the blackness of death. We have sent people there, and we know one day we must take that step into emptiness. We have seen, and we know. Do I tell you a lie?"

I shook my head. "No, I can't deny that. It's a place few people go before they die. When you've seen it, you are never the same again."

He leaned back and spread his arms. "We gonna get drunk tonight. At fuckin' last I meet a real man. These fuckin' *Vikings!*" He swept his arm around, taking in the bar. Several turned and looked resentfully at him. "They all fuckin' gay shit. They can't kill a cod fish. A man? Not one man among them. But you—" He gestured across the table at me like he was offering me his hand. "You are real man. SAS. I have lot of respect for SAS."

I could see something close to panic in Sigrid's eyes. I was seeing the first inklings of the craziness that she and her father had warned me about. He was getting excited, and it continued that could cost someone their life.

"I'm up for getting drunk. But I'm kind of hungry too."

Sigrid frowned at me and drew breath to mention the goat's leg I had just eaten. But she read my eyes, and I went on, "Has your dad got a kitchen here? Could you fix us something? While you're at it, Boris here and I can have a bit of guys' talk."

She nodded and stood. Boris leered at her. "But hurry back, baby. I'll miss you, and I am still waiting for your answer."

"You can wait another five days."

She turned and walked away through the crowd again. "So cruel," he said, smiling. "I must break her, make her mine."

I grinned at him. "She'll be one of how many?"

He laughed, leaned forward, and slapped me on the shoulder. "I don't know. I lost count."

I chuckled. "So Boris, if a guy wanted to do a little business around here, who does he have to see? Are you the man? Or is there a bigger man behind you?"

"You go straight to the point, eh? You not afraid."

"Afraid? What of? If I can make you money and make some of my own into the bargain, what's to be afraid of?"

He shook his finger at me in the negative. "You did not come here to write a novel."

"I came here to write my novel and to reinvent myself, Boris. And no sooner do I get off the boat than I meet you. We can't escape who we are, can we? Because who we are follows us wherever we go. I want to write my novel, yeah. But I want to feel alive again, breaking the rules and making money."

I held his eye, unwavering, as I said it.

He watched me for a long moment. "You are dangerous man," he said at last.

"Make no mistake about it, Boris."

"I should kill you."

"And miss all the fun?" I laughed out loud. "The way

you walked in here, in your silk Italian suit, the way you handle the island people—whatever you may say, these are tough men out here, and you treat them like shit. You ain't chicken. You got a pair of balls on you like an ox. Sure, I'm dangerous, and you know it. But you also know I can be useful to you. And you know I am not interested in New York, Los Angeles, Sinaloa. Those are not good places for me." I shook my head. "That's all bad news for me. I want my small island castle, my women, my local power. And I am more than happy to pay tribute to Rome."

There is a look a killer gets on his face when you do or say something he thinks is unacceptable. It's a barely noticeable shift, but suddenly there is contempt there. It's not so much contempt for you as contempt for those rules most people live by which say you shouldn't kill people, that people's lives are valuable. He's been there, he's done it, and it ain't so difficult. He'll do it again, to you.

I smiled at him and sipped my beer while I waited for his answer.

"And tell me, Saul, why do I want American Jew taking over *my* island, taking *my* money? Taking *my* woman?* You come here, drinking with my girl, making comments about my clothes. You fuckin' Jew SAS full of shit. I'm gonna kill you right now."

EIGHT

He was about to stand, but I sighed like I was being patient.

"If I am full of shit," I said with slow deliberation, still smiling, stemming his flow, "kill me tomorrow. Take me out in a boat and drop me in the ocean to die of hypothermia and drowning. It's a good end for a man like me. I'll fight you, I'll try and take you with me. I'll sure as hell take some of your boys with me. But I won't beg for mercy. If it's my time, it's my time." I pointed at him, my finger like a gun. "But before you do that, play the hand the Nornir have dealt you. I like you. You're a tough son of a bitch, and I respect that. You feel the same way, even though you hate me because I'm a Jew. You respect me. So play it out. What's the worst thing that can happen? I let you down, and you kill me. But what's the best that can happen?"

Death shifted out of his gaze.

"What are you talking about?"

"Let me ask you something. Who controls the traffic through these islands?" It was a long shot, but not as long as it seemed. It was calculated on an educated guess, and when I saw him narrow his eyes, I knew I'd hit the mark. I nodded. "It's what I thought."

He dilated his nostrils in an expression of contempt. "What you thought?"

"This"—I injected a little contempt into my own voice—"*secret corridor* of yours used to be controlled by Russia. The Russian Mafia backed by the ex-KGB elite backed by a crazy president who wants to recreate the Russian-Soviet empire. But then the CIA came along and, just as they lured the Soviet Union into a war with Afghanistan in the '80s, they lured Putin into a very ill-considered invasion of Ukraine. And they found a Ukraine far better prepared to defend itself than the SVR had led Putin to believe. And before they knew it, all of Russia's resources were being drained into an entrenched war over a few miles of Ukranian border, while its income was crippled by international sanctions. Suddenly the Russian Mafia is not as invulnerable as it used to be. It is a fact of nature, Boris. Where there is weakness, there is movement. Am I wrong? Did somebody else start to move in to the secret corridor and start muscling in on the trade with bigger and better ships?"

"How you know this?"

I wagged a finger in the negative. "That is not the question. The question is, what can I do about it? I refer you back to what I said to you five minutes ago. If I am full of shit, take me out in a boat and kill me, but before you do that, play the hand the Nornir have dealt you. What's the worst thing that can happen? I let you down, and you kill me. But what's the best that can happen...?"

"You are full of shit."

But he said it without conviction. He was thinking it over. He wasn't the only one. I had flown a kite on a hunch, and I had discovered something important about my target, Bogdan Novac. And on reflection, it made a lot of sense. That same reckless hubris which had led him to name his shipping company Sokol Shipping after the brigade he had led in Bosnia had led him to use his connections, his wealth, and his shipping company to move in on a weakened Russian Mafia and try to take control of the secret corridor.

I shrugged. "Maybe. But what have you got to lose?"

"So tell me, what is best that can happen?"

"I am a highly trained killer. You said so yourself. I was trained by the best. I tried living a normal life in suburban

New York, and I got bored—seriously bored—and that is why I am here." I laughed out loud. "Now no sooner do I get here than I meet you and discover I have chosen the world's most secret drugs corridor to write my novel on. Suddenly I feel alive for the first time in years. So here's what I suggest to you. Let me run this section of the corridor for you. I promise you, within a year you'll have more shit running through here than the Moscow sewage system. We will be selling direct into the UK and from there, anywhere you want. That island is an open door to Europe and the USA."

He was staring at me, thinking it over, wondering who the hell I was. It's an ironic fact that the thing people who live on the edge least like is surprises. People who live on the edge have a paranoid love of routine. They love giving surprises. They hate receiving them. I leaned forward and made the question deliberately confrontational.

"Have you got a problem?" Murder returned to his eyes, and he sat up straight in his chair. Right then I knew I was seconds from death. I smiled like he amused me. "No, Boris. What I am asking you is whether you have a problem on these islands. Who in this archipelago is trying to move in on your action?" I gave a small shrug. "Or is actually moving in on your action?"

He made the peace sign with two fingers. "Two," he said and pointed at me. "You are one of them. I don't trust you. I don't like you. Yes, I respect you because you are dangerous son of a bitch. But I don't like you."

"Trust me, play your hand like I said, and you will grow to love me. Who's the other guy?"

"Why? What will you do?" His tone was mocking but curious.

I shrugged and spread my hands. "If I can help out a new friend and at the same time show my good faith, I'd like to do that. After all, it's the kind of work I was trained in, and I was damned good, even by SAS standards. How many boats has he got? Two? Three? Four? What happens if a couple of them sink? Does he have a house in the islands? What happens if he has an accident, falls in the sea or falls backward onto a salad fork? I want to show good faith. I can always use the money, but above all I can use the excitement."

He spent a while frowning. This guy might have been as tough as reinforced concrete, but he wasn't smart, and he wasn't big league. He was a big fish in a small pond. After all, there might be tons of dope flowing through this channel, but as Jan and Sigrid had said, the authorities ignored it, for reasons only they understood. Eventually he said, "You will kill him?"

"That's what I said. I will kill him, and I will disable his fleet."

"You are big, crazy fuckin' American Jew."

I nodded. "Yup, that pretty much sums me up, Boris. That's me in a nutshell."

The timing was good. Jan and Sigrid appeared right on cue carrying trays of smoked salmon on toast, goat cheese, and dense rye bread. With it came more beer, and I poured myself and Boris a couple of shots of whisky.

I could see his boys and his driver watching us. They didn't look happy. They were too stupid to articulate it, but in their guts, they could sense a power shift going down, and they weren't happy.

I smiled at them like I was telling them they were right and shifted my gaze to Boris.

"Who's the guy? Where can I find him?" Before he could answer, I held up my hand and said, "Is it the guy with the house on Koloya Bay, or is it the guy he has placed to run the Ravnereiret?"

His eyes went real narrow. "How long you been here?"

"I don't know. Six or seven hours. I pay attention, Boris. That's what makes me dangerous. Is it him or not?"

"Yeah, is him. I don't know the guy in the house. I think he is weird fuckin' Italian Dante Gallo. Is the manager who runs old shit hotel Ravnereiret. There is gang there all the time with motorbikes. Some from the island, some from Norway. I don't know. But they givin' me problems. Every day more they are movin' in on my territory." He shrugged like he was going to make an objection that wasn't really worth making, but he made it anyway. "I don't know," he said. "I have no proof. But his boss is running small tanker ships out of Trondheim. They are going to Scotland, Liverpool, United States..." He did a slow wince and hunched his shoulders. "Maybe boss is just doin' legitimate shipping business, but this fuckin' crazy at the Ravnereiret is usin' him to make traffic and move in on my network. I cannot prove, but I know."

I knocked back my whisky, and he followed suit. I refilled our glasses. "Have you had a drop in demand?"

"You know so much, you know I have. He is movin' in on my buyers. I know it."

"Why don't you just go and kill him?"

"I send the boys to look. He has small army at the hotel-bar. Big guys in leather with big bikes. All with guns." He drained his glass again. "In Moscow they want to know what happens. Why drop in demand? They calling him Blue Tooth. I think is him."

"There is one way to find out," I told him. "If he disappears and demand rises again, it was him. Consider it a gift from me."

"There must be no comeback to me."

"Naturally. It will look like an Agency kill, steel jackets to facilitate later identification, no casings, use of a suppressor and no powder burns. I know what I'm doing, Boris."

He stared at me. I looked away and sighed, acting like I didn't give a damn.

"You keep me informed—"

"Fuck you." I said it to the wall, then looked at him with ill-concealed contempt. I didn't need to fake it. "I'll tell you when it's done if something more important doesn't come up. You don't own me, Boris, and you don't know who my friends are. Keep your balls in your frilly knickers, or I'll bust them off for you." Before he could answer, I stood.

"Where you going?"

"I'm going to the can. Is that all right with you?"

As I crossed the crowded floor toward the bar, I heard Boris shouting out for Sigrid, telling her to change the music. He wanted to dance. I found Jan pouring beers. He glanced at me and looked worried.

"I read you all wrong, pal. What game are you playing?"

"Don't ask if you don't want to know. And believe me, you don't want to know."

Sigrid pushed in next to her dad. Her cheeks and her eyes were aflame. "I thought you were different. I thought you were a man. But you...you are just like them! You know nothing about real suffering! About reality!"

"Can it till you know what you're talking about or you'll get us all killed."

She spat on the floor, turned, and set about changing the music to slow jazz you could dance to. I could still hear Boris calling for her. I said to Jan, "We need to talk."

"What about?"

"In ten or fifteen minutes, he's going to send his boys to ask where I am. You're going to tell him I asked you where the can was. You haven't seen me since then. Is that clear?"

He gave a single nod. "Where are you going?"

"I'm going to do you and your daughter a big fucking favor."

I turned and saw Boris draped all over Sigrid with his face buried in her neck. She had her eyes closed and looked like she was about to burst into tears. For a moment, I thought about going and killing him where he stood. Instead I turned and crossed the bar toward the door. Before I went out, I gave his boys the nod and pointed to the door. They frowned and shrugged. I gave my head a jerk that said I had something important, and if they were smart, they'd follow. Then I went outside into the freezing night.

The stars were ice crystals in a black sky. The moon, low on the horizon, cast a frozen, glistening path across the black ocean. I didn't have to wait long. I heard the door open and close behind me, and I turned to face them. There were two of them. One of them was the driver, and they were frowning at me, trying to make four out of six and six.

"What you are playing at, American?"

I took a moment to calibrate them. There was no

doubt all his boys were Russian special forces, and these two were no exception. The one on my right was the driver. He was lean, tall and blond, obviously of Russian descent. The other was Slavic or Cossack. Short and powerfully built with a broad face and slanting eyes. I shrugged.

"It was getting awful close in there. Hot. I came out for some fresh air to wake me up a bit. We drank a lot of whisky, your boss and me. I thought maybe I'd borrow his car and take a drive to clear my head."

The Russ guy slipped his hand behind his back. Two got you twenty he had a pancake and he was planning to plug me. I chuckled and jerked my jaw toward his hand.

"You figure that is a good decision? Boris and me have become good pals. You shoot his new friend, and he ain't going to be very happy with you."

His voice was real deep, like it belonged to an older guy.

"I am responsible for boss car. What you want? You talkin' shit. I don't like you, American."

"Hey, take it easy. I don't want nothin'. I am just out here chillin'. Me and your boss, we made good friends. I liked talking to him. He's a good man. So I am going to help him out with a little problem, and I guess you guys and me will be friends."

I stepped forward with my hand held out. "I'm Saul. Good to meet you."

They didn't move. The Russ guy said, "I don't like American shit."

"Aww, c'mon, guys. Boris is going to be unhappy if you treat his new friend and ally disrespectfully." I let my expression change, like I was some psychotic asshole who had attacks of extreme rage and violence at the word 'disrespect.' "You ain't disrespecting me, are you?"

I looked from the Russ to the Slav. They looked at each other. The Slav sighed and pulled a semi-automatic from under his jacket and pointed it at me. I didn't pause. I gripped the barrel hard. He must have weighed a good three hundred pounds, and I used every ounce of it to give myself impetus in the massive front kick I delivered with my instep to the Russ guy's balls. I felt them rupture and explode through the leather in my boot. His eyes went wide, and his face contracted as he doubled up.

I didn't waste time watching him. As soon as my foot touched the ground, I was pulling hard on the Slav again and smashing the heel of my left hand hard into the side of his neck, bruising his carotid artery and his jugular, affecting the flow of blood to his brain. His eyes rolled, and he gasped as he staggered a step backward. I stepped forward with my left and drove another massive front kick straight into his solar plexus. His lungs and his heart went into spasm, and he hit the dirt.

I pulled the Fairbairn and Sykes from my boot and drove it through the Russ guy's fifth and sixth intercostal deep into his heart. I leaned on it till he stopped kicking and jerking to keep as much blood as possible on the inside. Then I took the fob from his pocket and went over and did the same for the Slav. He didn't kick, and I figured I'd probably ruptured a blood vessel in his brain or caused a heart attack. It's what you get if you go pulling guns on people when all they want is to shake your hand.

NINE

THEY HAD A RANGE ROVER AND A WRANGLER. The fob was for the Range Rover. I climbed behind the wheel, hit the starter, and followed the rutted blacktop through the village, north and west.

What I had just done and what I was planning to do was—barring the absence of explosions—precisely what the brigadier and the colonel had told me not to do. The wholesale massacre of drug rings is not what you would normally call keeping a low profile. But the fact was I didn't give a damn. Drug dealers, in my book, are less than rats or cockroaches. Rats and cockroaches don't choose to be what they are. They are just following a natural drive. But the Borises of this world, the Bogdan Novacs and the Blue Tooths, they choose to be as they are, knowing they have options. They enjoy what they do, and for me, that means they have to be exterminated. But besides that, I was playing a hunch. It was a hunch that felt pretty solid to me.

Jan had been in the Marine Corps, and if I had read him right, he'd seen his fair share of violence, and he was no chicken. Now having watched Boris kill Olaf, he was having to stand back and watch Boris take not just the island of Odinnsey but also his bar, his hotel, and his daughter. To add insult to injury, he knew the cops would take no action, and there was effectively nothing he could do to stop it.

When he'd seen me on the ferry, he'd thought at first I was just another refugee from reality seeking somewhere to hide and write a second-rate book nobody was ever going to read. But then his instinct or his experience—or some combination of the two—had told him there was more to me than met the eye. More precisely, he had recognized the special operative and the killer.

And this was the part I had failed to read at the time. He wasn't warning me off Sigrid because of what Boris might do to me. He was urging me to get involved with Sigrid and protect her. He could see she was effectively about to be raped and reduced to the level of a gangland whore. He was prepared to give his life to save her, but when I turned up, he saw the chance of a variation in the plan. And that was OK by me.

But there was something else playing on my mind. It

was clear that Jan cared about his daughter, like any normal father would. And it was clear he hated Boris and hoped I would take some action. But there was something else, something I filed away for later because I could not quite grasp it.

Whatever the case, as it turned out, things had developed faster than he had expected. That was because though he knew soldiers and special ops, he didn't know exactly who I was. He didn't realize exactly who he had added into the mix. Like I said, as far as I am concerned, there is only one thing dope dealers are good for. There is no compromise. There are no mitigating circumstances. There are no deals to be cut. You choose to ride on the Hell Train, the fare is death.

Jan didn't know that. But knowing it or not, he had made a deal with the devil. I would free his daughter—and Odinnsey—from Boris and all the other scum that had accumulated along the secret corridor. But when I was done, I was going to want something in return from the US Marine Special Operative.

The road was long and straight and dark under a black sky. The blackness was like a solid substance all about me. The broad funnels of light from the Range Rover's headlights picked out nothing in that darkness but occasional rocks, dried, yellow grass, and the odd twisted, skeletal tree.

Soon I reached a desolate crossroads. A tall wooden

stake protruded from the ground in the amber glow of my lights. Three wooden arrows were nailed to it. One pointed the way I had come, and one pointed right, where I could make out the words *Kunna Point*. The third pointed left, and I could clearly see *Koloya Bay*.

I killed the headlights, and away in the stygian darkness, I could see a faint glimmer. I spun the wheel and headed toward that small glimmer at little more than five miles an hour, and I watched it grow from what looked like a distant star to a large, three-story building with a jumble of gabled roofs. Warm light flooded from its windows, and outside, I could see three trucks and at least a dozen Harleys.

A flight of six steps rose to a deck under a porch, and there I could see some guys sitting, drinking from bottles and smoking. I pulled in and parked. They went very still and watched me do it. I killed the engine and swung down from the cab and stood a moment looking at the four guys who were looking at me. I didn't know if they were Angels or bikers trying to look like Angels. They had their boots and Levis and black leather jackets. The older one had a long, straggly beard and long hair in a ponytail. The guy next to him was younger, maybe in his thirties. His hair was long and loose, and he had no beard. The other two were almost clones. The thought passed through my mind that they probably didn't look all that different from their Norse ancestors.

The guy with the beard spoke to me in Norwegian. "*Hva vil du, grisepenis?*"

The guy next to him gave a small rumble that was probably a laugh.

"I don't speak Norwegian. You have something to say to me, you'll have to say it in English."

He turned to his pal. "*Oh, grisepenis snakker bare engelsk.*" They both rumbled together, then the beard turned back to me. "What do you want, pig penis?"

"I want to talk to Blue Tooth. Is he here?"

"He don't talk to pig penis. So you can go and—"

"That's enough." I said it quietly so it would have more impact. "Mr. Gallo has sent me to talk to Blue Tooth. Is he here or not?"

The name made him stop. But none of them looked what you'd call intimidated. I put my foot on the first step, and by the time I'd reached the second, they were all four on their feet.

"You wait." It was the beard again. "I go tell Blue Tooth you are here."

"No." I shook my head. "You won't." They both frowned because what I had said didn't make sense. An uppercut is a very powerful punch. If you do it properly, putting your hips and your legs into it, it can be devastating. When you deliver it to a guy's weakest point while he is standing two steps above you, it can be lethal.

I didn't wait around to see the effect. I was under no

illusion. These were dangerous guys. So as Hagar the Horrible collapsed, wheezing, I took a step to my left and smashed a massive right hook into the side of his pal's left knee. Few things hurt as much as a damaged knee. All credit to this guy, he did not cry out in pain. But he did back off, dragging his left leg while he reached behind his back for his piece. I was moving faster than he was, and I was not in crippling pain. So I made the deck in a second and put another right hook through his head. He went down on his back, and I pulled the Glock from his waistband.

By that time, the other two were descending on me with rage in their faces. They took two slugs in the chest apiece.

I took the Fairbairn and Sykes from my boot and drove it into the second guy's heart. I cleaned the blade on his shirt and left Grisepenis and his pals on their way to Valhalla. I wasn't sure how the whole fighting and feasting with Valkyries would go down if you had no balls, but I wished them luck as I pushed through the door.

I'm not sure what I had expected, but this was not it. It was the kind of place I would have enjoyed if I hadn't been there on a mission of death. The music was Credence, the Eagles, the Doors, and Janis. The whole place was wood, and there were big logs burning in a six-foot fireplace. There were maybe twenty or thirty guys there drinking beer and whiskey. They all looked like

Ganger Rolf's crew reincarnated, they were all laughing and talking, and there were maybe a dozen or more girls, also in jeans and leathers, playing with the boys. It was noisy, and the two guys behind the bar were busy. Nobody seemed to notice me.

I looked around and saw the johns. A little to the right of the johns was another door that had a *No Entry* traffic sign nailed to it. Was it locked? There was no way of knowing, and in any case, I was on a roll. I had neither the time nor the inclination to be subtle. I crossed the room like I was headed for the john. When I got there, I moved over, took a hold of the No Entry door handle, and pulled. It came open.

While I was telling myself that made sense because either Blue Tooth or his men would be coming in and out during the night, I heard a low voice behind me. The words were Norwegian, but the tone was interrogative. I slipped through like I was in my own home and started to climb a flight of stairs to a landing and another door with another No Entry sign on it. Only this one also had a picture of a blood-stained axe underneath it.

I'd climbed five steps when I heard the door open behind me. I turned and smiled as a big guy with long blond hair and very pale blue eyes started climbing toward me, frowning in Viking. I smiled and said, "Do you speak English? Mr. Gallo asked me to talk to you about your connectivity."

He'd climbed three steps, staring at me like I was out of my mind, and I had descended two, talking like I was making sense. The last thing he expected was to have a razor-sharp six-inch blade rammed through his esophagus. But that was what he got. It's a wound that causes a very painful death by asphyxia, and I had nothing personal against this guy, so I slashed right and left and cut his arteries and veins, and death came to him all but instantly.

I sprinted up the remaining stairs to the landing and pushed through the door.

I found myself in a large, disordered office. The style was mock Tudor with timbered walls and heavy black beams under a white plaster ceiling. Two arched, leaded windows looked out onto blackness. There was a thread-bare burgundy sofa against the wall to my left. In front of that, there was an old coffee table with a silver box and a mirror on it. Maybe there was makeup in the box.

I glanced around and took in a Marshall amp, a Fender Stratocaster, and a Gibson SG. There were a couple of mic stands and a partially dismembered 1000CC bike engine on the floor.

At the far end there was a huge oak desk. Sitting behind it was a man who couldn't decide whether to be outraged or astonished. He had a mat of ratty black hair with gray streaks in it, and he didn't so much have a beard as his face looked like it was being invaded by cruel hair. He was wearing a black T-Shirt with the legend *Tors*

Hammer and a picture of him wielding a Gibson SG like it was a battle axe. His mouth sagged open, and I could see why he was called Blue Tooth. They might have called him Black Tooth instead.

Leaning against the wall scowling at me was a guy just like him, only his head was round, bald, and shiny. In a blue, scuffed armchair beside the desk was a third guy whose moustache was like a curtain in front of his mouth. His eyes were a pale blue and had a look that suggested his brain was in standby.

The guy behind the desk spoke like he was dragging his words through petrified nicotine.

"*Hvem faen er du?*" which I kind of got was *Who the hell are you?*

"I am looking for Mr. Blue Tooth. Is that you?" I smiled and pointed to the guy behind the desk. "Mr. Blue Tooth?"

The guy leaning against the wall muttered something about "*Skitt rumpehull!*" pushed himself off the wall, and moved toward me. "Who are you? What you are doing here?"

"Dante sent me?" I said it like it was a question. Like they should have been expecting me. "Dante Gallo? From Trieste?"

They were all three frowning, but I was less than two feet from the bald wonder by now. I knew that as soon as I acted, the weapons would be out. So it had to be fast and silent. I stepped in with my left foot bringing me in to less than twelve inches. I turned in my toes and drove a savage left hook deep into his liver.

The liver is one of the most painful places you can get hit. The pain isn't just crippling; if the blow is hard enough, it can kill. This guy was big and tough, and the scars on his face and arms said he'd been in his fair share of scrapes. But right then, he was doubled up and moaning like a girl. I shoved him to the floor with my left hand as I pulled my Sig with my right and put two slugs into the guy with the moustache. He looked mildly surprised and sank to the floor like he suddenly needed a quick nap. I couldn't hear Credence from downstairs, so I gambled that they hadn't heard the report from the weapon.

The guy behind the desk had by now opted for outrage. I pointed the weapon at his face and said, "I am going to ask you again, are you Blue Tooth?"

"Yes!" He said it like it was something he had achieved all on his own, with no help from nobody.

"Where is your safe?"

"You crazy pig skitt."

I went behind the desk and pistol-whipped him. Then I overturned his chair and threw him on the floor. He was fat and made a sizeable *whoomph!* I knelt on the small of his back with my left knee, placed the muzzle of the semi on the back of his left knee, and pulled the trigger.

He screamed. He'd been sitting on a cushion on his

chair. I grabbed it off the floor and smothered his face with it until the screaming had subsided. When he was panting and whimpering, I said to him, "Where is the safe, Blue Tooth? Think very carefully before you give me a stupid answer. Where is the safe?"

He was trying real hard to be a tough, badass guy, but I figured it had been a long time since he had hurt like that, and he was biting back the tears as he pointed to what looked like a set of wardrobe doors in the wall behind the desk. I reached for a pen and a scrap of paper and handed them to him.

"Combination."

His hand was trembling, but he managed to scribble the numbers down. When he was done, I told him, "Check it. You need to know this, Blue Tooth. If the safe doesn't open, you will never walk again. Are we clear?"

He nodded, and I went and opened the wardrobe. The safe was there along with two sports bags whose use I figured was pretty obvious. I hunkered down and spun the dials. The heavy door clunked and swung open. There was a lot of cash inside. Glancing through it, I figured over a million Norwegian kroner. I stuffed it in one of the sports bags, closed the wardrobe, and moved back to where Blue Tooth had started trembling on the floor.

I pressed the Sig into the back of his neck.

"You get one chance to live, Blue Tooth. Talk to me about Dante Gallo."

TEN

He was sobbing into the floor. Maybe I felt pity for him, but if I did, it was so fogged by the hatred I felt for predators and parasites like him who destroyed lives and didn't give a damn that it was more like I felt nothing.

"He owns this club," he said. "He's a very rich man. Very powerful. Maybe Mafia. I don't know."

"How long have you known him?"

"Couple of years. Please. I need doctor."

"You get a doctor and witness protection if you tell me the truth. You understand?"

He nodded with his eyes screwed up and saliva on his lips.

"Where is he from? What nationality?"

"I don't know, please. I don't know. He never talk about his self."

"You moving in on Boris' action? You shipping drugs to Europe and USA on his ships?"

"Yes." He nodded. He was weeping openly now, sobbing like a child. "Please, it hurt so much."

"Give me your cell."

He pulled it from his back pocket. I showed it to his face to unlock it and then set it to recognize mine. After that, I put the point of the Fairbairn and Sykes at the base of his skull, where it meets the vertebra, and thumped it hard with the heel of my hand.

"Now it doesn't hurt," I told him, "which is more than can be said for the thousands you've poisoned."

I made a quick search of the place and found a can of Zippo lighter fuel and a Zippo lighter with a skull and bones on it. So I sprayed his desk, the curtains, and the carpet and used the Zippo to set fire to it. It went up with a *woof!* A wave of heat washed over me. The flames swelled quickly into a big, warm blaze that reflected in the black windows as the flames crawled up the curtains. I took Blue Tooth's cell and filmed him and his pals where they lay dead among the spreading fire. Then I grabbed the bag of cash and walked out, closing the door behind me. I trotted down the stairs to the bar.

In the bar, the laughter and conversation had grown a little louder, more boisterous, and more drunk. The flames and smoke from the office were still contained upstairs. It would be a few minutes before they became detectable. The music had progressed to Joe Satriani and was melodic and bluesy. I stood at the door and looked around. The lights were dim, and everyone was half cut and stoned, so nobody noticed me. I shrugged, crossed the bar, and pushed out into the freezing night. I went and slung the bag of money in the back of the Range Rover, then looked back at all the parked vehicles, the trucks and bikes. I smiled to myself and remembered the colonel.

A fourth truck had joined the other three. It was a Ford Ranger pickup with the passenger side facing me. I walked over and hunkered down. The Ford Ranger has the gas tank on the passenger side, just behind the cabin.

There's a myth that if you fire a red hot slug into a vehicle's gas tank, it will ignite the fuel and explode. It's just not true. But what you can do is lie on your belly, take careful aim and put a 9mm slug through the belly of the gas tank so it starts to drain out. And that was what I did then on that dark cold night. And when the gasoline started to drain out, I took the Zippo I had just claimed as spoils of war from Blue Tooth, and backing up some, I lit the Zippo and tossed it into that pool of gas. It erupted like a small bomb, and the flames started licking at the perforated tank, heating and evaporating the fuel inside.

By that time, I was climbing into the Range Rover and pulling away with my lights turned off. Distantly I could hear shouts and cries. I saw flames illuminate my rearview mirror and then I heard the first of the detonations, drowning out the shouts and screams. There were four in rapid succession, and then a whole crescendo of them as the black sky turned flame orange.

The glow followed me halfway to Asketreby, and as I pulled up outside Sigrid's hotel, the western horizon was still glowing. I swung down from the cab, grabbed the bag of cash from the back, carried it into the hotel, and sprinted up the stairs to my room, where I dumped it under my bed.

Then I made my way down and crossed the square to park the Range Rover outside Jan's bar.

When I pushed in through the door, the mood had changed. There was no music, most of the patrons were gone, and Boris was sitting at our table with Sigrid and Jan, surrounded by his men. Everyone except Sigrid and Jan stood as I walked in. Boris looked real pissed. His cheeks were flushed, and his hands were trembling. He was about to speak, but I held up Blue Tooth's phone.

"Before you get your knickers in a twist, Boris, I borrowed your truck. You were busy getting romantic, and I thought I'd do you a favor to show my good will and bona fides."

He stared at me and then at the phone. I started to get bored, so I sighed, scrolled through, found the video, and handed it to him.

"It's Blue Tooth's phone. That's Blue Tooth on the floor with his two bodyguards. And if you feel like stepping outside instead of sulking in the bar, that glow you see on the western horizon is what's left of Ravnereiret."

He broke from staring at me like I was crazy, stared at one of his men like he was crazy, and jerked his chin at the door. That guy went and opened the door. He stood there, holding it open, and you could see the light reflected on his face and his jacket. He looked in at Boris and nodded.

Boris screwed up his face like a confused fist. "What have you done?"

"What you should have done a year ago or more."

His eyes went wide like he suddenly remembered something. "You killed two of my men!"

"They tried to kill me." I arched an eyebrow at him. "People who try to kill me tend to wind up dead." I let the words linger a moment. "They were incompetent anyway. You're better off without them."

I turned to Sigrid. She was watching me with absolutely no expression on her face. I smiled without humor. "What does a guy need to do to get a beer around here?"

She rose and went to the bar. Boris was outside still staring at the glow on the horizon. He and his man came back in, and the door slammed closed behind them.

"What have you done?"

I walked away from him to the bar, where Sigrid was

pulling beer from a pump into a tankard. When I got there, I turned to face him where he stood in the middle of the floor.

"What have I done? OK, if you'll take a moment to look at Blue Tooth's cell, you'll see that I killed Blue Tooth and two of his bodyguards. Before that, I killed four of his men in the parking lot. I killed another on the steps up to his office. I got Blue Tooth's phone for you so you can get the Russian Secret Service to do a forensic job on it, then I set fire to his office so that it would spread to the whole club, and I disabled his fleet of trucks and bikes."

Sigrid put the tankard of beer beside me. I smiled at her, took the tankard, and turned my eyes on Boris again.

"You're welcome," I said and took a long pull.

His voice was a rasp. "I said you were dangerous."

"And I told you you'd better believe it."

"You have started a war. You don't realize the repercussions this will have."

I snorted. "Grow a pair, will you. I started a war? I just got through telling you I destroyed his trucks and his bikes and took out Blue Tooth and a bunch of his men."

Jan spoke for the first time. He said, "You're out of your mind."

I turned to him, and suddenly the hot coals of rage were in my gut. "I'm out of my mind? If I'm out of my mind, what are you, Jan? I'm out of my mind because I see a threat and I go and take out the garbage. You? You see a threat and you lie down and spread your goddamn legs! Or you hope somebody else will take care of it, so long as they don't upset the damned apple cart. You want things to change but stay the same. So you tell me, Jan. Which one of us is crazy?"

His face flushed red. "You better shut your mouth."

"You going to shut it for me, tough guy?"

Boris was watching us with his mouth twisted into an ugly scowl and his eyes like cold diamonds.

"What is going on here? What are you talking about?"

I regarded him a moment and made no secret of my contempt. "So you're two boys down now, huh, Boris? Wherever you went, whatever you did, you had those same five boys with you." I drained the last of my beer and handed the tankard back to Sigrid. "But tell me, Boris, was that it? Was that the full size of your army?" I gave a laugh. "Coz I gotta tell you, man. When I went into the Ravnereiret, it was full. There must have been twenty guys there or more. They were drinking, laughing, having a great time. And then there was the big man, Blue Tooth, up in his office with his two bodyguards. He had a whole army there."

His skin was a sickly yellow. His voice was a rasp. "You son of a bitch."

I spoke very quietly. "Go home, Boris. The Ravnereiret doesn't exist anymore. Neither does Blue Tooth. But there are fifteen or twenty really pissed Hells

Angels out there, and they will be blaming you." I stepped forward and stabbed him hard on the chest with my finger. "And you owe me. You don't know it yet, but you owe me big time. And tomorrow I am going to call it in. You better be ready for me. Understood?"

"I will call Moscow..."

"And tell them what? That a filthy American Jew came and eliminated the massing enemy you hadn't told them about?"

"You can't do this..."

"I can't do what? Go to hell, Boris. Go home. I just destroyed your enemy, and tomorrow I will annihilate them completely. Just be grateful I'm on your side. Believe me, you don't want me as an enemy. Now get the hell out of here with your remaining men before I change my mind."

He backed up a couple of steps with outrage and terror struggling for control of his face. Then he turned and screamed at his men. It must have been Russian because I didn't understand it, but it was shrill and bordering on hysterical, like a parrot with a hornet up its ass.

At the door, he stopped and stared back at me. He'd gone silent, but his face was still screaming. He pointed a trembling finger at me. I spoke quietly. "Go home, Boris."

He went out and slammed the door behind him. The bar went silent. I felt a movement behind me and looked.

Sigrid had refilled my tankard and placed it at my elbow, but the expression of her face was one of disgust.

"Your beer," she said.

She came out from behind the bar, pulled on her coat, and left. Jan stayed staring at the door as it closed behind her. I took a pull on the beer while he stared. Finally he turned back to me and repeated his question. It seemed like the hundredth time. Like however much I spoke to him he could not hear me.

"What the hell have you done?"

"I did what you wanted me to do, Jan. But you should ask not what I have done but what I am doing. Because I only just got started."

"What the hell are you talking about? You think I wanted this? Do you realize how many people are going to die because of what you've done—"

I cut him short. "I already told you how many people have died. Let me ask you a question, Jan. How many people die every day because of that son of a bitch you were happy to watch fawning over your daughter? How many people will die if I *don't* do what I am doing?"

His jaw clenched hard, and tears sprang into his eyes. "You son of a bitch. Who the hell are you? What the *hell* do you want?"

"Don't ask if you don't want to know. I am going to do you a favor. I am going to do you the biggest favor anyone has ever done for you—more than you damn well deserve. I'm going to do it for Sigrid. Then I am going to disappear from your lives forever. But before I do that, I need something from you."

He looked resentful, but he asked, "What?"

"I need to know everything you know about Dante Gallo."

He narrowed his eyes at me. "You want to know about Gallo?"

"Yes."

"What the hell for?"

"I am not kidding, Jan. I am not buying the bullshit everyone is giving me that nobody knows anything about him. There are two bars on this island. You have one, and he has the other. There are three notable foreigners on the island: Boris, him, and you. I don't believe that you know nothing about him."

He looked like he was fighting the urge to pick up a chair and hit me with it.

"I'll tell you what I know about him. He's an old man." He seemed to hesitate a moment, nodding, glancing at a table like he was seeing a memory there. "Yeah, you're right. He came in here when he first arrived. He sat at that table." He pointed toward a table by the window. "And I recognized him. I recognized him the way I recognized you." His face twisted with anger. "Only where you are a soulless, damned killer, he is a soldier!"

He took a step closer and put his finger on my chest.

"And yeah, we swapped war stories. He's not Italian. I know the Italian accent—"

"He's from Trieste," I cut in. "The accent is different there."

"He's a Bosnian, you damned animal! He's a Bosnian who was kidnapped and tortured by the damned Serbs! And now you're going to go after him? Over my dead body!"

ELEVEN

I HELD HIS EYE FOR A LONG COUNT OF FOUR.

"It's a shame you didn't feel that strongly about protecting your daughter. Take your damned finger off my chest."

"He's an old war refugee, Saul. He's an old man who has come here to escape from his past."

He turned suddenly and walked away from me. He went behind the bar, grabbed a bottle of Johnny Walker, and poured himself a shot. He drained that and poured himself another.

"OK," he said, like he was agreeing with a voice only he could hear. "OK, I should have protected my daughter from Boris. But I stood here and watched him disembowel a man in front of a packed bar. We are all terrified of him. And it's not just what he might do to me; it's what he could do to her too. You don't know…"

He faltered. I raised an eyebrow at him. "What? I don't know what? What people like him are like?"

"I guess you do, at that. So you made him back off, and you're probably right: Blue Tooth probably got no more than he deserved." He held my eye and shook his head. "But Dante Gallo—" He shook his head. "That isn't even his real name. He took an Italian name, and he faked Italian papers and traveled here, to the remotest place he could find in Europe to try and escape from the horrors he had lived through in Serbia."

"Croatia."

"No." He shook his head again. "Serbia. He was a Bosnian in Serbia."

"You were there?"

"Yeah, I was there."

"Can you tell a Serbian accent from a Bosnian one?"

He studied my face a moment. "No. But I know a good man when I see one."

"What's his real name?"

He threw back the second shot and shuddered. "Adem Kodro from Mostar. Born in Mostar." He put down the glass and leaned with his hands on the bar, watching me. "Moved to Serbia when he was a kid with his family. When it was Yugoslavia, there was none of that shit. You had Serbs in Croatia, Bosnians in Serbia, Croats in Bosnia.

Nobody bothered about that shit. Until Tito died and all hell broke loose. His family was murdered, and he was arrested and tortured because they believed he was part of the Bosnian independence movement."

He eyed me a moment. "Why did you do this to Boris?"

"You feel sorry for him too? Is he just a victim of the collapse of the KGB?"

"Enough is enough, Saul. Just answer my question, will you?"

I took a pull on my beer. As I set down the glass, I said, "How many reasons do I need? If Blue Tooth's Hells Angels blame Boris for what happened tonight and they hunt him down and kill him, they'll have done the world a favor. More than that, I saw the look on Sigrid's face when he was dancing with her. I saw the look on her face when she told me she'd have no choice but to accept and be his girl on this island. So I did it for her. And I did it for you. I'm not a father, but I can imagine what it's like to see your daughter subjugated to that, knowing she's going to be raped repeatedly and to feel powerless to do anything about it. And I have one other reason."

He was watching me carefully. "What?"

"I want to see if Dante Gallo, a.k.a. Adem Kodro, will respond."

"What is your obsession with that man? He's a guy who has dragged himself out of the jaws of death and despair and recreated himself on this island, while at the same time creating a thriving enterprise on the mainland. Give the guy a break."

"How long has he been here?"

I saw his eyes flit over my face. "Couple of years, maybe three. You think he's a goddamn war criminal, don't you?"

"Do you know he isn't?"

He nodded. "Yeah. You are way off base. He is one of the kindest, most human people I have ever met."

"So what's he doing with a bar like the Ravnereiret, where they try to knife you if you want to go in and have a beer?"

"Are you always that quick to judge? Did you stop to think that maybe Blue Tooth was running the joint and Adem had no idea how he was doing it? Because Adem, once he had handed over control for the running of the place to that animal, just wanted to stay safely behind the walls of his house."

I sighed and shook my head at my beer. "You're telling me that this guy, who has been so badly traumatized by the war, would hand over the running of that bar to a criminal like Blue Tooth? You don't think he'd have a kind of sixth sense about who he was dealing with?"

"No." He shook his head. "No, I don't. I think he put his shipping company in the hands of a board of directors in Trondheim and the bar in the hands of a strong person-

ality who took charge. I think *that* is who Adem—Dante!
—is. I think he is a tired, damaged old man who wants to
hide from bastards like you! I think he's the kind of man
who younger, aggressive people like Blue Tooth take
advantage of."

I sighed. I knew well enough how easy it was to draw a
misleading profile on somebody. In a full court of law, in
the glare of the public media, with a jury exposed to all the
facts, an innocent man might go to the chair, or a guilty
man might walk free. How much harder was it when security services, some with dark, vested interests, were
involved. Both the brigadier and the colonel had warned
me that it was not a confirmed fact that this was Novac.

"I need to meet him."

"No way. You can put a gun to my head. I won't
do it."

"Listen to me—"

"No!"

"*Listen to me!*" He glared at me across the bar, and for
a moment I saw the Marine, and I wondered what had
happened to him, how he had come to this island, how he
had come to a place where he could watch Boris fondling
his daughter and do nothing.

"Jan, if I wanted to kill this guy, whatever his name is,
I would not need an introduction from you. That is not
why I am here."

"Why are you here, then?"

"That is none of your goddamn business, and believe me, you do not want to know."

"You're a killer."

"That's yesterday's news, Jan." I pointed at him. "And while you're on your moral high horse, don't lose sight of the fact that your daughter is not being raped tonight because I stopped that from happening. I didn't need that complication, nobody paid me to do it, and in the process, I have blown my cover and made a lot of enemies—some of whom I would rather have as friends."

He sighed again and rubbed his face with his hands.

"You owe me," I told him.

"OK." And then, "What do you want with Adem?"

"I don't know. Maybe nothing. That's why I need to see him and talk to him. I don't expect you to like me, Jan. One thing I can tell you is that I'm not here to make friends. But you owe me, and tomorrow you're going to owe me more. I will call in the favor, and you will pay."

"You make me sick." He said it quietly. "You, the people like you, you're the reason I left the Marines. You take what should be noble, and you make it filthy."

"Right. Stop before you give me an epiphany, Jan."

"Fuck you. What happens tomorrow? What are you going to call in?"

I thought about it. "I'm not sure yet. All of this has come out of left field, and I need to think. But you just remember something, Jan. And make sure it's at the front of your mind when you get up in the morning. This guy who makes you sick, this guy who makes all noble things filthy, is the reason your daughter was not raped tonight. Think about that tonight as you slip into your virtuous sleep."

I left him scowling sullenly at my back as I walked out of the bar. A moon was rising low over the horizon, casting a liquid silver path over black water. The air was freezing, promising snow, but the sky was clear. With practically no light pollution, the stars were bright, and the Milky Way was a rich nebula across the heavens.

I made my way toward the hotel, shuddering in the cold. I needed badly to sleep and to plan my next moves. So far, contrary to everything I had ever been taught, I had improvised on the spur of the moment. All things considered, it had played out better than I had a right to expect. But the next move would be critical. I was far from clear in my own mind that Dante Gallo—or Adem Kodro—was in fact Bogdan Novac. I didn't rate Jan as an infallible judge of character, but neither was he stupid. He had Kodro down as a vulnerable old man and nothing more than that. Which meant that before I took another step, I needed to be sure in my own mind of who I was dealing with.

———

I was up late the next morning. I showered for twenty minutes and changed my clothes, then went down for breakfast at nine. The light had changed. The bright, cold sun had been replaced by heavy, gray clouds. I found Sigrid in reception, watering some potted plants. She was in a pair of jeans and a heavy Aran sweater with her hair tied in a knot behind her neck. Her eyes said she hadn't slept.

"Good morning." She glanced at me but didn't answer. "Any chance of some breakfast?"

"Of course." She said it without looking at me. "What will you have?"

"Eggs, bacon, toast, coffee?"

She put down her watering jug and walked quickly into the dining room to push through the swinging doors into the kitchen. I sat at the nearest table and waited. The coffee took just a couple of minutes. She brought a Moka pot and a demitasse. The eggs and the bacon came out five minutes later with toast and butter. She set the whole lot on the table and sat opposite me. The expression on her face said she was about to spoil my breakfast.

"I don't know where to begin," she said, which, by definition, was not a great start. So I glanced at her and decided I would begin with the bacon.

"I would like you to finish your breakfast and then leave. There is nothing to pay. I would just like you to pack your things and leave, please."

I sat back and watched her while I chewed, swallowed, and sipped my coffee.

"I can understand that," I said as I set down my cup. "But you haven't thought it through, have you?"

"I certainly have—"

I gave my head a single shake. "No, you haven't. And please, let's not get into a 'yes I have, no you haven't' match. Hear me out."

"I want you to leave. There is nothing to think—"

"Your father is alive today, and you were not raped last night, because of me."

I speared a piece of bacon onto a piece of toast and dunked it in the yolk. I watched her while I chewed. When I'd sipped some more coffee, I went on.

"You're trying to find a way of refuting that, but you can't. Boris turned up here, at your hotel, looking for you. When he was told you were at your dad's bar, he went there looking for you. He brought five men with him. Stop me if I make a mistake anywhere along the line."

She didn't say anything, so I went on.

"He came here for one particular reason. He had no intention of waiting five more days for what he wanted. Men like Boris don't wait in line, and you know it. And they don't listen to reason. Ask Olaf. Oh"—I clicked my fingers—"you can't because he's dead. You saw how he was coming on to you, and you know damned well what his intentions were. Now I have a question for you. How much do you think your dad was going to tolerate? I saw your face when he was dancing with you. You looked like you were about to burst into tears. I wanted to go over and smack him, and I don't even know you. What do you think your dad was feeling?"

She still didn't answer, but her eyes shifted to the table.

"Whether you hold a knife to a woman's throat or you quietly threaten to kill her family, it is still rape. Just because he persuaded you that the best way to avoid violence was by giving in to his demands doesn't mean it's consensual." I leaned forward. "And if I see that, so does your dad. And if it sickens me, I can only guess at how your dad feels about it. Now you have to come down to reality and ask yourself, if Boris had forced you to take him to your room last night, what do you think your father would have done? What would you have done if it had been your daughter?"

"I..." She trailed off and sighed. I didn't think she was going to come out with anything I didn't know already, so I went on.

"I am not justifying what I did last night. I don't need your blessing or your dad's. But the sickening, disgusting action I took last night was to get Boris in my debt and deplete the number of men he had available to him, just in case your dad did something before I got back."

The change in her expression was subtle, but it was unmistakable. Her jaw sagged slightly, and she frowned.

"There are few things in this world, Sigrid, that disgust me as much as a drug dealer. They destroy millions of human lives every year by robbing those people of their wills, their lives, and ultimately their souls. But I did not come here to eliminate Blue Tooth or Boris. I did what I did last night because any asshole could see Boris was intent on forcing you into becoming his sex slave and humiliating your father into obedience. I also knew that would be your father's breaking point, and that would cost him his life. Do I need to go on? What would you be, Sigrid, after watching your father murdered in his bar, the way Olaf was, and then being raped by the man who killed him?"

She closed her eyes, and her lip began to curl. I saw a tear spill from the corner of her eye.

"I'm nearly done," I said. "I am going to ask you to consider one last thing. What do you think Boris would do to you if I left now? How many hours do you think you and your dad would have left?"

I finished the food on my plate and drained my coffee. "I won't be leaving, Sigrid. Not because I am a sickening piece of filth but because I decided last night to free you, your dad, and this island from Boris and Blue Tooth and those who follow them. I will finish what I have started. Then," I said, with more bitterness than I had intended, "you can celebrate my departure and mourn the happy days of your special relationship with Boris."

She met my eye. Her cheeks were wet. "That was unfair," she said.

"Was it?" I shrugged. "I don't get the luxury of complaining about unfairness. I am just a sickening bastard who got used to life being unfair a long time ago." I stood. "I'll be gone in a couple of days."

TWELVE

I crossed the area of dirt they called a square and pushed into Jan's bar under the lowering, snow-cold clouds. The place was empty, but Jan was behind the bar polishing glasses. He watched me approach. His eyes were not friendly.

"I need a couple of things, Jan."

"Good morning to you, too."

"I need a strong, black coffee, and I need a car. Is there some place here I can rent a four-by-four?"

He didn't answer. He dropped the dishcloth on the counter and went to the Gaggia machine. He took his time loading it and setting the cup. While the black trickle fell into the cup, he reached in his pocket and pulled out the keys to his Toyota and tossed them in front of me.

"I can't say I like you, Saul. It's hard to like somebody

who holds up a mirror to you and shows you what a shit you've become. But I respect you, and everything you said last night..." He trailed off as he brought over my coffee. "That was all true. If you hadn't intervened, he would have forced Sigrid, I would have tried to do something, and they would have killed me. They'd probably have forced Sigrid to watch, too. So I owe you."

I gave it a moment, then nodded and told him, "Thanks. I appreciate it."

"How long do you need it for?"

"Maybe a couple of hours."

"You said you were going to call in the favor. Is this it?"

"No."

He prepared himself a milky coffee while I sipped mine. The Gaggia screamed loudly in the dark room. Outside, desultory voices sounded as they passed the window.

I asked, "How many men has Boris got?"

He closed his eyes and stood like that for a long moment. "I left the Marines because I was tired of the killing. I escaped to this remote, frozen island to escape from the killing. Will it ever end?"

"Jan," I sighed loudly, staring down at my cup. "Well over one and a quarter billion people are going to die by 2045."

He managed to scowl and make his eyes go wide at the same time. "What the hell are you talking about?"

"That's the number of people who are over sixty right now in the world. By 2045, they'll practically all be dead."

"Jesus Christ, Saul!"

I ignored him and went on. "Every day about one thousand two hundred and fifty people die as a result of homicide, and that's not taking into account armed conflicts and terrorism. People die, Jan. There is nothing we can do about it, but we can at least try to make our existence useful and meaningful for other people. How many men has Boris got with him at his house?"

"More killing. I don't want any more killing, Saul."

"But you want somebody to free your daughter Sigrid from that bastard. You want to clean the sewer, but you don't want to get your hands dirty. Well, that's OK. That's why I am here, Jan, to take out the trash. How many?"

He opened his eyes and started polishing the bar. "I don't know for a fact, but probably eight."

"He had five with him last night. Three more than that."

His face hardened. "You killed two of those. So he has maybe six now."

"Yeah, who knows, Jan? Maybe those were the two who were going to hold you while he disemboweled you."

He stared at me. It wasn't gratitude I saw on his face. "How do you do that?" he said. "That brutality?"

"It's not hard." I drained my coffee and set down the cup. "I just think of what these people do to their victims, of all the lives they destroy, of all the hope they rob from kids, mothers, children. I am capable of a limited amount of compassion, Jan. What I have, I keep for people who are worth it. People who traffic drugs, murder children, rape mothers, they're not worth it."

I left Asketreby along the broad, dirt track that served as the island's only road bigger than a goat track and headed west and a little north, toward Kunna Point. I passed the crossroads I had seen the night before, and in the distance, I could still see the trails of smoke from the burned-out club.

Instead of turning left, I turned right and headed for the most northerly point of the island. Here the landscape was rockier, with large mounds of boulders peppering the landscape, towering over the yellowed grass against the heavy gunmetal sky. The road wound and twisted, and where the east of the island was flat, here the road climbed and plunged down slopes into stark valleys, with the gray ocean in the distance.

Boris' house was startling when it came into view. At first it blended into the landscape, but then it was suddenly there, gleaming on a cliff, overlooking the ocean. The walls were white, with huge plate glass windows. It was very modern, on three floors, set back behind a six-foot wall, and as I approached, I saw that there was what looked like a path and steps cut into the rock, leading down to a bay at the foot of the cliffs.

After about five minutes, the road came to a halt just outside his house. There was an intercom set beside a large, gray steel gate. I climbed down from the truck and pressed the call button, and a voice that was as inviting as the Russian Steppes in January, only less exciting, asked me who I was.

"Saul Goldman. I'm here to see Boris."

The gate buzzed and rolled slowly back. I got back behind the wheel and followed a gravel track among yellow grass and bare rocks to the desolate house that over-looked the windswept cliffs. If Frank Lloyd Wright had wanted to express terminal depression, he would have designed this house.

I pulled up onto a bare concrete forecourt beside the Range Rover I had driven the night before and swung down from the cab. In front of me was the sheer, white façade of the house, with a single door and no windows. The plate-glass windows, from what I could gather, gave on to the ocean and road.

There were two guys sitting at a table beside the door smoking and playing cards. They had automatic rifles leaning against the wall and when they looked at me, they got the kind of Russian expression you get on your face when you've eaten too much kholodets. They didn't say anything. They just watched me and waited. The door buzzed, and they got to their feet. I approached them, wondering if I was going to have to kill them then. I paused a couple of feet from them, within striking distance. The one on my left had a scar across his left eye. The one on my right was younger and had pockmarked skin from adolescent acne.

"I'm here to see Boris. You going to step aside and let me through?"

Acnevich answered. "He's waiting for you in sauna. You go there."

I pushed between them into a large hall with huge terracotta tiles on the floor. Dull gray light filtered through passive panes of glass in the wall on the right. The walls were whitewashed, and a blond pine staircase climbed up along the right wall to a broad galleried landing. The ceiling, three stories up, was supported by heavy, raw tree trunks that still had the bark attached. It was strangely Scandinavian, yet out of place on this island.

Ahead, beyond the staircase, there was a broad arch. Through it I found a broad living room with glass walls on three sides. In the far wall, fitting into the plate glass, was a huge stone fireplace that looked like it might be five hundred years old. The floor was strewn with goat skins, and there was heavy, calico furniture scattered apparently at random.

A door in one of the glass walls opened out onto a covered patio where I could see a large hot tub and beyond that a large, pine outhouse which I figured was the sauna.

Boris was in the hot tub with three Scandinavian beauties with platinum hair, very white skin, and very blue eyes. They were so alike for a moment I wondered if he had cloned them in Moscow. Each of them had a glass of champagne in their hand.

Sitting in a chair by the sauna was another guy who'd eaten too much boiled cabbage. He was looking at his cell phone with his rifle leaning against the wall. He glanced up at me as I stepped out. A fourth guy was sitting in a white plastic chair over on the left on a patch of artificial lawn. There was a white wrought iron table there with a tray of drinks on it. That was four guys. I wondered where the other two were.

I stepped out into the gloom of the terrace. Boris grinned a grin that was as fake as it was forced. He waved at me. "Good morning, Saul, take a seat. You want a drink?"

The girls were looking at me and laughing, like he'd said something real funny. I ignored them along with his offer of a drink.

"You recruited an army since last night?"

He curled his lip. "This is what you have left me. Because of your crazy actions last night, I have to have maximum security now."

I folded my arms and leaned against the glass wall.

"Quit griping, Boris. You know I did you a favor, and I'm not through. By the time I'm finished, you'll own this corridor."

He grunted. "Or you will."

"I'm not interested in the stress. That's for empire builders like you. All I'm interested in is easy money."

He raised his voice and shouted at the guy sitting at the table.

"*Dimitri! Get coffee!*"

Dimitri brushed his shaggy blond hair from his eyes and said something in Russian that sounded like, "*Konechno boss.*" I figured it meant, "Yeah, boss," or whatever the Russian gangster equivalent was. He went inside, and I sat at the table. I watched the girls for a moment. They were quiet now, smiling, sipping, graceful, and shiny in the bubbling water.

"You're an ungrateful man, Boris," I said. In my peripheral vision, I saw him stare at me. "A guy could feel unappreciated."

He rose from the tub, causing bubbling tidal waves that made the girls scream. He stepped out and grabbed a towel which he dabbed himself with all over. When he was half dry, he pulled on a huge, red toweling bathrobe. He stepped into a pair of sandals and flip-flopped over to the table.

Before he sat, he said something to the guy with the

automatic rifle. It had lots of Rs and Ls in it. The guy nodded and waved the girls out of the hot tub. They complained a lot, wrapped themselves in fluffy towels, and went inside. When they'd gone and the guy with the assault rifle was back, he sat and spread his hands at me.

"So tell me."

I raised an eyebrow at him. "Again?" I sighed. "I went to some lengths last night, Boris. I killed ten men all told—"

"Two of them mine!"

"Yeah, two of them were yours. And I burned down a club full of Hells Angels and killed the director of the club. And I did all that because I wanted to get your attention. Have I got it?"

His eyes became hooded. "You got it."

I held up two fingers. "I want two things from you, Boris. One, I want a job worthy of my skills. And two, I want to know everything you can tell me about Adem Kodro."

"This again." His eyes went real narrow. "Why? Why this obsession with Dante Gallo? I thought you was here to write a fuckin' novel!"

"That does not concern you. I have personal reasons that don't concern you. You don't want to help me, that's fine. I'll go elsewhere."

His eyes remained narrowed, and unconsciously he began to dab his face with the sleeve of his robe. "Personal reasons, huh...?" After a moment, he shrugged and pulled a face. "When he came, few years ago, he makes friends with Jan. He tells Jan first he is Dante Gallo, from Italy. But then him and Jan start drinking, telling war stories, and then he change his story. He is not from Italy, he is from Bosnia, or Croatia, one of those countries, and he is victim of Serbian atrocities. His name now is Adem Kodro, but don't tell nobody."

"Jan told you this?"

"Jan tells me everything. He knows he must tell me everything."

"So Adem Kodro is a Croat?"

"I don't know if he is Croat; maybe he's a Bosnian or Serbian or some shit from Monte Negro. For us, it was easy. They were just Yugoslavian. They are all the same. But they think they are different." He shrugged elaborately. "He makes his business in Trondheim with shipping." He spread his hands. "What else can I tell you?"

"His name. His *real* name."

"How do I know?"

"You run this section of the secret corridor. It's worth many, many millions, and you control it. A new, mysterious, reclusive guy arrives and buys a house on the island. It turns out this guy is running a shipping company bang on your corridor, and he has an employee who is running a club for Hells Angels. To cap it all, you find out from your lackey Jan that this guy is from the former Yugoslavia, and you don't contact your ex-KGB pals back in Moscow and ask them who this guy is?"

He puffed out his cheeks and spread his hands wide. I went on.

"You start to notice a drop in demand for your trade, and *still* you don't ask your pals in Moscow to look into this guy."

"Yeah, yeah, OK. I made some inquiries."

"And?"

"Kodro. His name is Kodro, Adem Kodro. He is from Bosnia. He escapes, but he has friends." He screwed up his face like he'd bitten into a lemon. "'Don't touch him.' You know? That's what they tell me. 'Ignore him. Make like he is no there.'"

"But he's encroaching on your trade."

"That's what I think. And I tell them this. 'Since he comes here, demand is less!' But they tell me, 'No. Is not him. Ignore him.'"

"So if it's not him taking your trade and satisfying the demand, who is it?"

"I don't know. How can I know? I ask Moscow, and they say, 'Don't worry about it.' Don't worry about it? I am losin' money, stuck on this shit island in the snow and the ice! Don't worry about it? But Moscow say don't worry, I don't worry."

"You're full of bullshit, Boris."

But I said it absently because I wasn't sure it was true.

It didn't make sense any way I looked at it. He was scowling at me.

"One of these days I am gonna break your arms and your legs, and I am gonna throw you in the sea, *sukin syn!* And maybe that day is today!"

THIRTEEN

I GAVE HIM A SMILE I HOPED WOULD LINGER IN his nightmares.

"*Sukin syn*? That's one of the few things in Russian I know. Son of a bitch, right? That's funny. It's what your mother called my father when he refused to pay her for her services. You want to break my arms and legs? Call your boys and do it now before I break your neck."

He raised both hands and closed his eyes. "Relax. We just talkin', right?"

"Wrong. You are talking a lot of crap. I am not just talking. Now if I am going to be any use to you at all, Boris, I need to know. Is there anybody else on this island, Balkan or East European, Rumanian, Albanian, anyone who might be connected to a mafia somewhere?"

He made a face like I was crazy. "No Balkan mafia, no

Albanian mafia, no Rumanian mafia. Just me and the fuckin' Blue Tooth Angels—"

I allowed irritation to show in my face. "Come on, Boris! I'm not doing this because I like your pretty face! Let's get real! Have you been told by Moscow to back off from Kodro? If so, why? If he's involved with the Albanians or the Rumanians, what I did last night could be bad news. I need you to lay it on the line for me."

His face said he was getting confused. That wasn't of itself a bad thing, but I had to be careful not to push too far. His eyes narrowed. "You came here to write a novel? You don't come here to write a novel. Why you are here?"

"Jesus, Boris. You're a bit slow sometimes. Did anybody ever tell you that? Seriously? I'm on a contract, Boris! I am a contract killer, and I am here on a contract. OK? Now I did what I did last night, and it was the right thing to do. Blue Tooth was part of the contract. But I am beginning to wonder now. Have I been given all the intelligence I need? Was something left out of the brief? Are these guys connected to the Albanians or the Rumanians? I can tell you, if that is the case, then that is real bad news. How many guys you got here?"

"Six," he said, and his eyes were flitting all over my face. "I had eight. You kill two of them."

I sighed and ran my fingers through my hair. "I'm going to the john, Boris. Call your contact in Moscow and find out who this guy is. I need to know that before I do another thing, right?"

I went inside feeling his eyes on my back. I knew he had decided to kill me, and he was just considering the angles. Dimitri was inside, and I said, "WC?" and used some fairly explicit sign language. He jerked his head that I should follow him. He led me to a flight of stairs and pointed up.

"Zoli, up." Then he shouted something up the stairs that sounded like, "*Otvedi etogo sukina syna v tualet!*"

I figured Zoli was upstairs, and he now had instructions to take me to the can. I told Dimitri "OK" and gave him the thumbs-up. Then I climbed the curling flight of blond pine stairs to an upper floor where the plate glass walls allowed a sweeping view of the island and the ocean and the low, bellying clouds. Scattered flakes of snow had started to drift down from the heavy, gray sky.

There, sitting on a straight-backed chair was a long, thin guy with short hair, crooked teeth, and dispassionate eyes. He got to his feet and led me down a short corridor. There he pointed to a door at the end and said, "*Tualet.*"

I grinned and gave him the thumbs-up and started to talk word salad at him. "Like French, huh? And the effigy of the overlap on the underside is what? How do we come to find that other side of nothing? Right?" I spread my hands and gave a small laugh as I hunched my shoulders. "I mean, what *is* the sound of one hand clapping?"

I waited for a reply, watching him intently. His face was screwed up into a frown, and right then, nothing made sense to him. So I shifted my right foot forward a couple of inches, gave it a little twist inward, and drove a powerful right hook through his jaw. I caught him as he went down and dragged him into the bathroom. There I laid him on the floor, then slipped the razor sharp blade of the Fairbairn in behind his left collarbone and drove it down the full six inches to the hilt. His feet did a little dance, and his hands twitched. When he'd stopped, I removed the blade and wiped it on his shirt, but there is practically no bleeding from that wound.

I stepped out into the corridor. Boris had said he had six guys there, which fit with what Jan had told me. There had been two on the door and two by the pool, Zoli made five, so the sixth guy must be up here somewhere.

I took a stroll down a small maze of corridors with parquet floors. I opened three doors as I went and found bedrooms that had been slept in and then cleaned by maids. The fourth door I opened, I found a guy lying in bed with his back to me. He seemed to be asleep. His clothes were on a chair up against the wall, and his Taurus semiautomatic was hanging at the end of the bed.

I stepped in quietly and closed the door. He didn't stir. I took two long strides, and with my left hand, I pulled back the duvet. Simultaneously I rammed the Fairbairn and Sykes into his back at the level of the sixth intercostal. I felt the two ribs crunch as the blade forced them apart and drove deep into the heart. He went into spasm, and his legs kicked like he was trying to run. Then his breath croaked as it left his lungs for the last time, and he became still.

That was two upstairs, which left four downstairs. Two at the door and two at the sauna. I went down the stairs quickly and quietly. Dimitri was out on the covered terrace again, and through the glass, I could see Boris getting dressed. I slipped into the entrance hall and went fast to the front door.

I stepped out into the cold, and they both looked up from their card game. I smiled in the kind of friendly way that made them sneer with contempt. I said, "Is this unexpected?"

There was no way of telling whether they understood or whether they spoke English. Their faces were blank with a hint of hostility. I rammed the Fairbairn into the back of Acnevich's neck, severing his spinal cord while he sat motionless, goggling at empty space. What happened next took less than a second. The guy across the table with the blind, scarred left eye goggled as best he could with just one eye and started to get to his feet. By that time I had let go of the dagger and stepped forward with my left foot. From there, I rammed my thumb into his blind eye.

It was a nauseating feeling, but it allowed me to drag him to his feet while he whimpered and gripped my wrist.

Using the full impetus of my movement and his combined, I smashed his head against the wall and drove two massive left hooks into his liver. I dropped him, stamped on his neck to kill him, though he was probably already dying from a ruptured liver, and wiped my thumb on his sheepskin jacket.

The rearguard was dead. And the main army was cut off from any reinforcements. It was now just a case of striking the death blow.

I went back inside and found Boris and his two boys in the living room. Boris didn't look happy. He eyed me as I came in, and there was murder in his eyes.

"I been talking to people in Moscow."

I got a twist of adrenaline in my gut but hid it. "Yeah?"

"I ask them about Dante Gallo, Adem Kodro. You know what they tell me?"

I folded my arms and frowned at him like it was a stupid question. "Clearly not, Boris. What did they tell you?"

"First he starts screaming at me. Ignore this guy, forget him, how many times they gotta tell me, leave him alone..."

"That's interesting."

"Yeah, real interesting. But more interesting is when I tell him to calm down, because reason I am askin' is an American here getting real interested in Dante Gallo."

I gave my head a small shake. "That was not a smart move, Boris. What did he say?"

"He say this guy is from former Yugoslavia, he done a lot of favors for some of our friends, and he is protected."

"That's helpful. Did he tell you his real name?"

"Yeah, his name is Fuck You, Mr. Saul Goldman!"

"Really? That sounds more Anglo-Saxon than Serbian."

That was probably what the colonel would have called facetious, and she would probably have agreed with what Boris observed next. He pointed at me and curled his lip and said, "You full of shit! You lie, and lie, and lie! And only reason anybody believe you is because *you so crazy, nobody can believe...*"

His voice had got steadily more shrill, and his face had turned puce. His mouth worked, but he'd screamed himself into a syntactical minefield and didn't know how to continue. His two boys were frowning at him like they were waiting for a cue. I knew that when that cue came, it would be the cue to kill me. What he didn't know was that the two boys he had with him were his last two boys.

"You're right," I said. "It has all been lies. My name is not Saul Goldman, I am not a Jewish attorney from New York, and I have no desire to join your organization."

He was nodding as I spoke. Like he had been really smart and blown my cover.

"So! I knew it. Who are you?"

Dimitri and his pal trained their weapons on me.

"My name is Harry Bauer. I am a professional assassin. My contract is not for you, but now that you know who I am, I will have to kill you."

His face screwed up with rage and he screamed, "*Ubey yego! Ubit' sukina syna!*"

I don't speak Russian, but you didn't need to be a linguist to know he was screaming *Kill the son of a bitch.* So before he'd made it to 'son of,' I had stepped forward, laughing and saying, "Come on! Don't be so sensitive!" and put both arms around him in a big, Russian bear hug. To say the situation was bizarre would be like calling Mount Everest a hill. Dimitri and his pal were waving their automatic weapons at me. I was clinging to Boris like he was my long-lost brother, and Boris was screaming, pushing, and struggling to get away from me so his boys could get a clear shot. It was like some weird, ancient ritual dance with the four of us shuffling around in circles, all shouting at the same time, going nowhere.

Boris was shouting at his boys to shoot me. Dimitri was shouting at Boris to duck or move, and I was shouting at everybody to take it easy. It seemed to go on for a long time, but it was probably just a couple of seconds, as long as it took me to slip my left arm around his throat and pull the Sig from my waistband. I put two rounds through Dimitri's chest. For a split second, I saw panic in his pal's eyes as he tried to get a bead on me without killing his boss. After that, my round tore through his face and blew his brains out the back of his head.

I shoved the Sig back in my belt, put my right arm behind Boris's neck in a choke hold, and began to squeeze.

"Freeze or I'll crush your windpipe."

I gave it some pressure, and he began to slap my arms. I eased up and took the Sig from my belt again. I pressed it into the small of his back and said, "Get on your knees."

Boris had started to weep. "What do you want from me? I have lots of cash in the house. We going to take it to Guernsey for cleaning. You can have. Just take. We got lots of shit here too. Take! You can sell it. Couple of million bucks."

"Where is the cash?"

"Upstairs, in office."

"In the safe?"

"Of course."

"Walk."

He led the way back up the stairs. We moved past the vast glass wall. Outside, the snow was starting to fall heavier. We moved down a parquet corridor and came to a stripped pine door. He went through, and I followed him. It was a surprisingly spartan room. It was large. One wall was all glass, and in good weather, it would have been sunny and bright. There was a large, pale oak desk, a couple of armchairs, and a credenza with a tray of drinks.

Most important, in the corner behind the desk, there was a safe the size of a small suburban house.

I gave him a shove. "Open it."

He half-turned, sobbing badly. "Listen to me…"

"Open it three, open it two, open it—"

"*OK! OK! OK!*" He was screaming, running forward, arching his back away from me like he could avoid the bullet that way. He scrambled to the safe, fell on his knees, and began to turn the knobs with trembling fingers. When he finally opened it, it was full of cash.

"You got two million dollars here. You have it. I can get you more. Don't kill me. Please, I am beg you. Please."

"I told you I want two things from you."

"Yes, anything, please."

"I want Dante Gallo's real name."

"He is protected. Russian mafia and Iran MOIS have agreement. He must not be touched."

"I am going to ask you one final time, Boris."

"Bogdan! His name is Bogdan! Bogdan Novac! He is protected. I cannot touch him! You cannot touch him. Nobody can touch him!"

So it was him.

"OK, Boris. You done good. I told you I wanted two things from you. One was Novac's name. Now I want the other thing."

"What? Anything. I give you information. I give you

two million bucks. I can get you more. What else you want?"

"I want you to pay for all the misery and suffering you have caused. I want you to pay for the children and young adolescents you have hooked on drugs and destroyed their lives. I want you to pay for the hundreds of women you have forced into prostitution. I want you to pay for all the young men you have forced into the production of drugs. I want you to pay for the thousands, maybe millions of lives you have poisoned."

He had turned to stare up at me. His face was transfigured. His mouth was twisted open, and his face was wet with tears.

"*How?*"

"By understanding this. All the misery, fear, and grief you are suffering now is what each one of them has felt for years because of you."

I shot him with that thought in his mind. The Buddhists believe that the last thought in your mind before you die is important because it conditions your next life. I don't know if that's true. The universe seems cruel enough to make us come back over and again. So maybe they're right. If they are, then maybe Boris would come back as a decent human being.

Maybe.

FOURTEEN

I took the bags of cash out to the Toyota and stashed them on the back seat. The flakes of snow were still gently falling, but it wasn't sticking yet. After that, I took my time finding the keys to the Range Rover and the BMW and used a length of garden hose to empty the gas tanks into a couple of plastic buckets, a large pressure cooker, two large pots, and a few other containers I found about the place. Once that was done, I collected up all the cell phones, flash drives, and computers I could find —ten cells, one flash drive, and one laptop—stashed them all except Dimitri's in a large refuse sack, and dumped them with the cash. Then I spent five minutes dowsing the inside of the house with the gasoline I'd recovered. After that, I left Dimitri's cell on the coffee table in the living room, made sure all the doors and windows were tightly closed, and went to the kitchen. There I opened all the taps on the stove to release the propane gas through the burners.

Finally I went and climbed in the Toyota and rolled out of the big, iron gate. I drove maybe a quarter of a mile, pulled over, and killed the engine. I figured I'd need at least twenty minutes for the gas to accumulate and fill a large house like that one, with lots of open space. So I climbed out and sat on a rock, gazing out at the cold gray sea under that cold gray sky, and listened to Credence on the Toyota's sound system. I see the bad moon arisin', I see trouble on the way.

By the time his old hound dog was chasin' down a hoodoo, I looked at my watch, took my cell, and called Dimitri. I half smiled to myself, half expecting a voice to come on and say, "Dimitri can't come to the phone right now..." It wasn't funny, really. Death should never be funny. Dimitri was some mother's son, as was Boris, as were all the kids they had destroyed between them.

There was a strange optical illusion for a second as the house trembled and seemed to go out of focus. Then the vast glass walls glowed orange and exploded, sending molten glass spraying into the air. Then the house was engulfed in flames. For a moment, I wondered, if I had saved more lives than I had taken at Boris' house, would that make what I had done morally justified? I get deep like that sometimes. I shrugged and climbed back in the truck and made my way slowly back toward the crossroads among the steadily falling snow. On the way I figured Billy Shakespeare probably got it right anyway. There is no right or wrong, but thinking makes it so.

The brigadier had told me that.

I came eventually to the desolate, barren place where the road divided. Over on my right, a mile or more away, lay the smoldering remains of the Ravnereiret Club. Behind me the burning shell of Boris' house. I stopped the truck and sat staring at the wooden post. For some reason, I remembered Oppenheimer's words when he watched the first atomic bomb tests. He quoted from the Bhagavad Gita, where the god Vishnu tells Arjuna, "Now I am become Death, destroyer of worlds."

Had I become Death, the destroyer of worlds, or had I just killed the god Vishnu? Either way, I was screwed. I decided I was not ready to face Novac right then. My head was not clear, and the plan, which was supposed to be a simple case of detection and execution, had turned into murder and mayhem.

I spun the wheel and headed back toward Asketreby. The snow was falling heavier now and beginning to stick, making it harder to follow the road, which was hard to follow at the best of times. Several times I came off and had to spin the wheels to get back on again. But finally I saw the cluster of buildings that was the village come into view. By the time I pulled up outside the hotel, the snow was a couple of inches deep. I heaved the bags out of the truck and carried them inside. Sigrid was behind the desk and stood as I came in. She saw the bags and frowned.

"What's that?"

"The spoils of war." I hesitated a moment. "Boris won't be troubling you anymore. Neither will I. I should be gone by tomorrow."

"Saul, what have you done?"

I gave my head a small shake. "That doesn't concern you. It's best you don't know." I moved to the stairs and stopped. I looked back at her. "Sigrid, ninety-nine times out of a hundred I would tell you, in a situation like this, you'd be smart to phone the cops. This time is the exception that confirms the rule. Don't do it."

Her eyes went wide and her jaw set. "Are you threatening me?"

I gave a small laugh. "No. I am no threat to you. I have all but screwed up the job I came here to do by trying to save you. It would be stupid to threaten you after all this, wouldn't it?" She frowned, trying to make sense of my words. I sighed. I felt suddenly weary. "No, I think Boris owned the local cops. I think they were on his payroll, maybe Blue Tooth's as well. You know nothing, have seen nothing and heard nothing. Trust me on this."

I climbed the stairs to my room and dumped the bags of money under the bed with the one I had taken from the Ravnereiret Club.

I pulled my cell from my pocket and called the brigadier.

"Harry, where are you?"

"Odinnsey."

"Any progress?"

"Yes and no. I think I might have fucked up, sir."

"Are you all right? You sound odd."

"The situation was more complicated than we anticipated, sir. I responded using my own judgment and…" I took a deep breath. "Let's just say the colonel would not approve of what I have done."

"Oh, I see. What have you done? Did it involve an explosion?"

"I burned down a Hells Angel club last night, and today I blew up a house belonging to a Russian mafia drugs trafficker."

There was a long silence. Finally he said, "And what about Bogdan Novac?"

"I have all but confirmed it's him. The Russian mafia and the Iranian MOIS protect him. He is apparently not to be touched. Boris Petrov, the mafia guy, confirmed the guy on the island is Bogdan Novac, but he was told by Moscow to leave him alone. He is protected."

"That's something. So what are your plans?"

"I need to see him and talk to him. I'll probably do that tonight. If I'm satisfied, I'll take him out and go home."

Another silence. Then, "You don't sound right, Harry. Do you want to abort?"

"No. I'm fine. I'm just tired. I need to tell you. There's what they call the secret corridor. It comes up from Thailand, Afghanistan, and Turkey, through Russia to Belarus and Poland, and then into Scandinavia. These islands of Norway provide a gateway across the North Atlantic to the UK, Iceland, Greenland, and Nova Scotia. We're talking about heroin and opium and all their byproducts. There were two guys on this island, Boris Petrov and some Hells Angel by the name of Blue Tooth. They were both involved in trafficking along that secret corridor. There should have been a conflict between them, but there wasn't."

"You're talking about them in the past tense."

"Yeah. I killed Blue Tooth last night—"

"When you burned down his club."

"Right, and I killed Boris today."

"When you blew up his house."

"Yeah. There are things that don't make a lot of sense. My experience of Hells Angels is that they hang out in deserts, near beaches, and close to bars. They don't hang out on small, Norwegian islands where there are only two bars and practically no people. And from what I hear, the club actually belonged to Novac."

He grunted. Then, "So why are you uncertain about him? Everything seems to point to him being our man.

Perhaps he contracted the Angels through this Blue Tooth because he was planning to wipe out Boris Petrov."

I took a deep breath and sighed. "Yeah, I'd be inclined to agree with you. Only there are two people here I trust, up to a point. He's an ex-Marine, and she is his daughter. They say he's a good man, a soldier, a tired, broken old man trying to escape from people like me. They say his name is Adem Kodro, from Mostar, in Bosnia. They say they know him, and he's a good man."

"Psychopaths are often more believable than sane people."

"I know it. That's why I need to see him and talk to him."

"Yes, fair enough. I agree." I heard him sigh. "Harry, Jane is going to be very unhappy about this."

"Neither of the events can be traced to me."

"Was it absolutely necessary?"

I hesitated a moment, then said, carefully, "To an outside observer it would look like gang warfare. The cops, once they get involved, would not believe one man alone could cause so much damage. It looks like an attack and retaliation."

"All right..."

"And if I take out Novac, if it's him, it will look like an accident, or suicide. As the colonel instructed."

"Was it necessary?"

"Yeah. He was going to rape the daughter and kill the

father. The cops have been instructed to stay away from the island and give these bastards a free hand. I couldn't stand by and let it happen."

"No, Harry. I know. That's not who you are. Let's leave it at that. Least said the better."

"Thank you, sir."

He hung up, and I sat staring at the phone, thinking.

I went down the stairs. Sigrid watched me cross reception but didn't say anything. I stepped out into the snow and drove the truck the hundred yards across the square which was now carpeted in white under a heavy, sagging sky that was growing dark. I parked outside the bar. Light was filtering through the window like it was evening, though it was only midday. I pushed through the door and let it swing closed behind me. There were a couple of guys up at the bar hunched over a couple of beers. Jan was at the cash register, counting bills. He looked up and watched me cross the room to where he was at. I slipped the keys to his truck across the counter.

"Boris won't be giving you or Sigrid any more trouble."

"What have you done?"

"That's not your concern, Jan. I need to talk to you and Sigrid, together."

"When?" He gestured. "I have the bar..."

"In an hour. It won't take long. Ten, fifteen minutes."

He nodded, then looked down at the keys. "Thanks," he said, then looked at me and said again, "Thanks."

I nodded and made my way back to the hotel. She wasn't in reception, so I climbed the stairs up to my room. As I let myself in, I was suddenly overwhelmed by a sense of exhaustion. It wasn't a physical tiredness. It was a weariness inside.

I stripped and stepped into the shower. I turned the water to scalding hot till it made me shout, then turned it to freezing cold, scrubbing myself with soap and shampoo, as though I could wash away all the blood that had accumulated on my hands and body over the years.

Eventually I turned off the water and stood a moment looking down at the white, tiled floor. In my mind I could see Boris, staring up at me with terror twisting his face. It was a vulnerable, childlike expression. And I put a slug through the back of his neck. So what gave me the right to live and decide that he should die?

I walked into the bedroom toweling myself dry and stopped dead. Sigrid was sitting on the bed, watching me. Her expression was impossible to read.

"I don't do the three monkeys."

I frowned. "What?"

"Don't see, don't hear, don't speak. That's not my style." She waited a moment, watching me. "I see," she said. "I hear and I speak."

"You've taken me out of context. You have also caught me with my pants off."

She didn't say anything, just stared at me like she was waiting for something.

"I said if the cops, or some type of law enforcement come asking questions, the best thing for you and your dad is to say you know nothing."

I went to the chest of drawers and pulled out a pair of jeans. I dropped the towel beside her on the bed and pulled them on. As I zipped them up, I told her, "You know that. You understood me when I said it. So what's the real reason you're here?"

"Tell me what you've done."

"I killed Boris."

"Just like that. Other people go to the store and buy bread. You go out and kill somebody. What about his men? Will they be turning up looking for—"

"I killed them too."

She screwed up her face. "You killed his men?"

I sighed. "That's a stupid question, Sigrid. And you don't need to know. I killed them, and I burned his house down, with all his dope in it. But if people come asking questions, you know nothing, you understand that?"

She was only half listening, and her eyes told me she was about to ask the question she'd come here to ask.

"Why did you do it?" I drew breath, but she went on.

"You said downstairs that you had screwed up the job you came here to do so you could save me."

I opened the wardrobe and pulled out a shirt. "I came here to write a novel, remember?"

"Don't bullshit me."

"I'll have to leave the island now."

"Listen to me!"

I turned to look at her as I buttoned up my shirt. She was getting mad, and I could tell she wasn't going to give up.

"Let's pretend I am stupid enough to believe you came here to write your novel, let's assume I am stupid enough to believe you found me so charming and beautiful you were powerless to resist and had to save me from a fate worse than death with Boris. Even then, going to Boris' place and shooting him would have been extreme." She sat shaking her head. "But you didn't do that. You played him and Blue Tooth so it would look like a gang war, and then you *massacred* them. You burned down Blue Tooth's club and then you burned down Boris' house and killed him and all his men." She sat shaking her head again. "And having done that, you come and tell me you screwed up the job you came here to do so you could save me? What am I supposed to believe?" She leaned forward, staring at me. "You have shown zero signs of any interest in me. Who the hell are you? Why the hell are you here, and above all, what the *hell* was your original job you came here to do? Exterminate the whole fucking island? What?"

"OK," I said and sighed. "I'll tell you."

FIFTEEN

"I GET PAID TO TAKE OUT THE TRASH. NOW I AM going to make something real clear for you, Sigrid. Every word I tell you increases the risk to you and your dad. I don't want to tell you. But there is one thing more dangerous than my telling you, and that's you nosing around trying to find out for yourself. Now for the last time, forget it. I'll be gone by tomorrow."

"No. I want to know what you came here to do and why you massacred these people."

I spoke with more savagery than I'd intended. "Do you want your dad to get tortured and killed?"

"Of course not!"

"Then when I have told you what I am going to tell you, you leave! You forget it! Understood?"

She nodded. "Yes."

"Boris and Blue Tooth were both involved in trafficking drugs from the East, across Russia and into Europe and the States. I have seen what these people are prepared to do to promote their operations. I've seen what they do to the growers and the people who make the drugs. They are basically slaves, and any sign of weakness or disobedience is punished with torture and death. I have seen what they do to their rivals, I have seen how they treat the women and children they traffic as sex slaves through Poland, and finally I have seen their victims all over the streets of New York, San Francisco, and every major city in the West. As far as I am concerned, these people have abdicated their status as human beings and have no rights."

I walked to the window and looked out. It was getting dark, and the rooftops were getting heavy with luminous snow.

"I know your dad is basically a good man. And I like you." I turned to face her. "You're wrong about my having no interest in you. I have. But with my life, I can't show it. In another life, in another reality, I would probably have let you know. But I am not a man you want to get close to."

I took a deep breath and went on. "When I saw that creep slobbering all over you, when I saw the expression on your face and I saw your dad suffering but unable to do anything about it, I decided I had to act. Direct action would have had consequences for you and your dad. So it had to be oblique."

"You're kidding me."

I frowned. "Why?"

"You'd known us like five hours, and you did all that for us?"

"Mainly for you. Why wouldn't I?"

She laughed an ugly, incredulous laugh. "What was it, love at first sight, or what?"

I spoke with a bitterness that surprised even me. "No," I said, "it wasn't love at first sight. I just don't like to see assholes like Boris raping young women I have taken a liking to. Though if the expression on your face is anything to go by, that makes me an asshole too."

She closed her eyes and took a deep breath. After a moment, she said, "I'm sorry. That's not what I meant. It's just..." She spread her hands and opened her eyes wide. "You killed like fifteen men. That's a massacre, Saul!"

"Every single one of them was guilty of collaborating in the destruction of thousands of lives. I am not going to apologize for ridding the world of them."

Her voice came as almost a whisper. "That's not the way to do it, Saul."

"OK." I shrugged. "Show me, and if it works, I'll do that instead. But I have to tell you, Sigrid, that the way you were doing it didn't seem to be all that effective. He was all over you like a rash. He and Blue

Tooth were trafficking freely, the cops had been warned off the island, and you were a couple of hours from getting raped. And your dad was probably going to get shot or knifed in the process." I gave a dry, ugly laugh. "I mean, the fact is, there was enough trash here to turn it into a massacre, and that's got to tell you something, right?"

"This is madness." She said it half to herself, but I answered anyway.

"And what you had before wasn't? It's not madness so long as they cover it up and hide it?"

She sighed. "OK, you made your point, Saul."

I eyed her over for a moment, wondering what she was made of and whether she would help me. Finally I said, "I saved your father's life, I saved you from rape, and I may well have saved your life too. Now I need to call in the favor."

There was a look of disgust on her face. "So that's what this is all about."

A small, hot pellet of anger ignited in my belly. "Are you out of your mind? I have easier ways of getting favors, and most of them don't earn me the contempt of the people I help."

Again she closed her eyes and sighed. "I don't..." She sighed again and ran her fingers through her hair, still with her eyes closed. "I don't feel contempt for you, Saul. It's just—" Now she opened her eyes to stare at me. "It's a lot to take in. Maybe in your world, this is normal. But out here…" She trailed off.

"I need you to introduce me to Dante Gallo."

Her face went like stone. "I will not be a party to your—"

"I just need to meet him and sit and talk to him."

"He's an old man."

"Yeah, I know, Sigrid. So is Radovan Karadzic, so is Ratko Mladic, but growing old doesn't wipe out what you did when you were younger. It doesn't exonerate you, and it doesn't change you. You can still be a sadistic son of a bitch at eighty, eighty-five, and ninety."

She got her feet and stepped close to me. "He is not a son of a bitch! He is a sweet, gentle old man."

"That's how people who'd met him used to describe Franco. Franco was responsible for the murder of two hundred and fifty thousand people *after* the civil war had finished. His Foreign Legion was instructed to rape, pillage, and terrorize every village they marched through."

He face flushed with anger, and she stabbed her finger into my chest. "I know him, and you *don't!*"

"Exactly!" I half-shouted it into her face. "That is why I need to meet him face to face and talk to him. Because I am not sure if he is the man I am looking for!"

She went quiet. "That's why you're here. You're like one of those Nazi hunters."

I sighed loudly. "Something like that."

"And who do you think Dante is?"

"Bogdan Novac, born November 8th, 1955, which makes him about seventy now. He was a sergeant in the Sisak Police Department and headed up a paramilitary group called the Hawks. They were responsible for massacres in at least three villages near the border with Bosnia, one of which was particularly horrific."

I watched her face. She watched me back. I was wondering if she'd tell me to stop or to go on. She did neither. She just waited.

"The Croatian cops at Sisak suspected there was a Serbian paramilitary group based in a village in the hills called Babina Planina. So the Hawks, headed by Novac, were dispatched there in a number of Land Rovers and four armored cars equipped with heavy machine guns.

"There were some thirty to fifty heavily armed men. They rounded up about a thousand villagers in the town square and began to systematically murder the children." She gave a startled little cry and put her hands to her mouth. I paused a moment, then continued. "It didn't take long for the mothers to break and give Novac the information he wanted: the names of the members of the paramilitary group and where they were based.

"But once he had that information, Novac didn't release the villagers. He ordered the execution of the entire village. Many of them were tortured before they were killed, and their bodies were hung from lampposts as a warning to others. The victims included men and women in their eighties, mothers and their children."

She sat and scowled down at her hands in her lap. "I don't believe... I won't believe that Dante could do something like that."

"I hope you're right. You need to understand something. I don't want to kill an innocent old man who is simply trying to escape from his ghosts. That would make me as bad as the trash I'm out to eliminate. But there are others in my organization who have become so jaded they don't care anymore. And if I go back with an inconclusive report, next time they might send someone less scrupulous than me."

I shrugged. "More to the point, Sigrid, there is nothing to stop me breaking into his house and taking him out. But I don't want to do that. I want to know if he is or if he is not Bogdan Novac."

"And what if he is?"

"Then I'll have to make a decision. But you won't know anything about it. You won't be any part of it."

"Jesus Christ." She whispered it half to herself.

"Does he live alone? Who does he live with?"

She looked me over for a couple of seconds. "I'm not sure. He has a guy who drives him around on the very rare occasions he goes out. He has a woman who cooks and cleans for him. That's about it. He might have a family member there, but I'm not sure."

"What about Blue Tooth and his Angels? That was Gallo's club. Your father seems to think Blue Tooth was just taking advantage of him."

She gave a small shrug. "I guess that sounds about right." She smiled with an ironic twist. "I can't imagine poor old Dante setting up anything like that. Honestly, when you meet—"

She stopped dead.

"You'll do it then."

"Do I have any choice?"

"Of course you have; you just make it much more difficult for me."

"You don't understand."

"I don't understand what, Sigrid?"

"You don't, how could you...?" For a moment, she seemed to be talking to herself. "It's why we came to this island in the first place." She glanced at me suddenly. "Did Dad tell you?"

"Tell me what?"

"Why we came here."

I shrugged, a little confused suddenly. "He said he came to get away from the ugly shit he'd experienced in the Marines and to write his novel."

She got to her feet and came and stood in front of me. Her face was a mix of confused emotions. She was frowning, like she wanted to be mad at me, but her eyes were telling me something different.

"Dad is wanted for murder in Colorado."

It came out of left field, and for a moment, all I could do was frown at her. She waited, searching my face. "We were driving through on our way to San Diego. We stopped at a place called Hartsel. It was just like a dozen houses, a general store, and a kind of bar and grill. I was a young teenager. Mom was—" She hesitated a moment. "Mom was really beautiful.

"We stopped and went into the grill. Everything was fine. They were friendly, and we ordered some burgers and Dad had a club soda. Because he never drank while he was driving. And we were nearly finished and about to pay up and leave..." She seemed suddenly to go into a kind of trance, like she was talking to herself. "I think so often, if we had just arrived five minutes earlier and left five minutes earlier, none of this would ever have happened..."

"What happened, Sigrid?"

"Four guys on bikes turned up."

"Bikes?"

Her mouth moved, but she had to take four runs at it before she said, "Harleys. They were bikers..."

"Angels?"

She nodded. "They had their full patches on their jackets. We were paying, and they were ordering beers. One of them, a fat guy with a big beard, made some comment about Mom. We ignored them and were turning to leave when a younger guy, he had long red hair and freckles, he stepped away from the bar and said to my dad, I remember it so clear, 'Hey, the man's talkin' to you. Show some respect.'

"I remember Dad stopping and talking quietly to them. I know he hated the Hells Angels and any criminal organization, but he wanted to avoid trouble because me and Mom were there. So he said something like, 'I have a great deal of respect for you guys. Me and my family are just leaving.' Something like that. But the fat one said, 'Well I won't take offense, but to make up for your insult, I am going to need your cute wife to do me a little favor in the back of your truck."

She stopped and took a step closer to me. "My memory gets a bit vague at that point. I remember my dad walking toward the fat one. It was like slow motion. I could hear Mom screaming. I remember Dad hitting the fat one over and over. The other three were on him. I remember the fat one went down. Then another one went down bleeding. There was a lot of blood. The red-haired one rushed at Mom, screaming at her. And she was screaming. I remember. Then Dad went after him, and after that, I remember the red-haired one lying on the floor, and there was so much blood everywhere. I'm not sure what happened to the fourth one. I think he was on the floor too, and there was lots of blood."

She had her hands on my chest. Unconsciously I had taken hold of her shoulders.

"What happened to your mother?"

She looked at me suddenly, like the question was a crazy one. Her eyes flitted over my face. She went to answer three or four times until she said, "She died."

"The red-haired Angel?"

"No. She never... She got ill after that happened. The doctor said she was traumatized. She went to bed and never got up. Then one night she accidentally took too many pills. I don't remember anything else. Except the police started looking for us, and we left. And we came here."

"Hells Angels."

"Yes."

"That's quite a coincidence."

"That's what I said to Dad. But he said I shouldn't read anything into it."

I took a deep breath. "Listen. I had no idea about all this. Leave it. I'll find another way—"

"No, you're right. You need to know. We need to know."

She took her cell from her pocket and stood a moment looking at the screen. Then she leaned her head against my chest. "It's been such a long time since I talked about that. It's been so many years."

Without thinking, I drew her close and put my arms around her, stroking her hair. She made no sound, but I felt her tears soak slowly through my shirt. After a time, she looked up into my face.

"You saved my dad. You saved me. I can't believe I've been so ungrateful..."

"Hey, take it easy. I had no idea all that had happened to you."

Her body pressed up warm and close against me. I shook my head. "Don't do this, Sigrid. This is a bad idea..."

"You're not bad like him." Her eyes were huge and dark and blue. "You wouldn't do the bad things he has done."

"No..."

"You will be gentle and kind."

Suddenly my belly was on fire. It could not be right, I told myself, that killing was permitted but love was not. I crushed her to me, and her mouth sought mine. She came to me easily, and then we were entwined on the bed, tearing at each other's clothes.

SIXTEEN

THE GLASS IN THE WINDOW WAS BLACK. THE wind had picked up, and through the triple glazing, you could hear the occasional howl as random white flakes danced across the blackness. I lay staring at her back, where she sat on the end of the bed and pulled her cell from her jeans pocket. She didn't call right away. She sat looking at the screen. Eventually she sighed and called.

She held it to her ear. After a while, she turned to look at me and put it on speaker, so I could hear the message that said he either had his phone switched off or he had no signal.

She pointed at the window. "It's the weather. It affects the signal when it's like this."

She hung up, then went to Whatsapp.

"Hey, Dante, how are you? The weather is turning

pretty rough, and we were wondering if you're OK or if you need anything. Do you need us to bring you anything? Let me know, OK?" She sent the message and sat staring again. "I feel such a hypocrite and a liar. Jesus! I'm luring him to his death!"

I sighed and sat up. "Don't get carried away. I just want to talk to him. I hope as much as you do that this is a case of mistaken identity."

I sat up and pulled on my jeans and a shirt. She glanced at me. "I should take some food over to Dad. You want to help me, and we'll eat over there in the bar?"

I agreed, and ten minutes later, we went down and loaded up her truck with roasted goat, potatoes, and vegetables, and drove the short distance through the snow. Once we were inside and I had deposited a load on the counter, Sigrid told me to get myself a beer while she and Jan arranged the food in the kitchen. It was as I was cracking the bottle behind the bar that I saw the shadows move against the glass in the door. The door opened, and four figures hunched through among a swirl of snowflakes. They stood looking around, stamping the snow from their boots and beating it from their shoulders. Then their eyes fell on me behind the bar. They paused and nodded a couple of times.

They were Hells Angels.

I poured my beer and watched them cross the floor. "Good evening."

They glanced at each other without expression, like they were confirming something. The closest one was probably six three with his boots off. He was strongly built and had a big chain around his neck that hung down to his belly. He had long, uncombed blond hair and a beard Hagar the Horrible would have been proud of.

"*Gi meg fir øl, grispenis.*"

I gave a small shrug and smiled politely. "I don't work here. I'm just a friend. Do you speak English?"

They all looked at each other and laughed but not in a way that made you feel like joining in. The guy on the chain's right was shorter but more powerfully built, and he had a big ring through each ear and one through his nose. When he leered, he had both front teeth missing. "*Snakker vi Engelsk?*" he asked his pals, and they all rumbled like Thor playing with his hammer.

On the chain's right, there was a tall, lean guy with a long red beard and dangerous, pale blue eyes. He leaned on the bar with hands you might use for quarrying granite.

"I speak English." He said it in a voice like a geothermal disturbance. "My friend Olaf told you give us four beers, pig's penis. Now you have heard it in English, you can go and get the beer, pig's penis."

I gave my head a couple of small shakes and drained half my beer. "No, see, I don't work here. So I guess your *friend*"—I gave it a laden emphasis that made them all frown—"Olaf will have to go and get his own pig's penis." I pointed at the guy with the ring through his nose. "Is he the pig?"

Nobody rumbled.

Olaf answered in a voice that sounded like they'd been sandpapering his larynx.

"We will talk about who is pig in a little while, *fitte*, when you are on your hands and knees, crying like a girl. First you are answering some questions."

"Oh, am I? OK." I drained the remains of my beer and set down the glass. I belched. "Go ahead."

Red Beard said, "You were at Ravnereiret yesterday in the night?"

"I can't remember. Was that when your pal Blue Tooth got killed?"

They didn't answer. They stood and looked at me, and their faces said they really wanted to roast me over an open fire. I snapped my fingers and pointed at Red Beard. "My turn. I have a question for you. Did you guys work for Blue Tooth? Or do you work for Dante Gallo?"

"You are very stupid man." It was Olaf with the sandpaper voice. "Come, I show you about pig."

He moved to the flap and raised it to get in behind the bar. Meanwhile Red Beard put both hands on the counter and vaulted over it while Nose Ring and the fourth guy went after Olaf. That left me with Red Beard and an empty bottle of beer.

I moved fast. I smashed the bottle into the side of his head as he landed. A couple of the shards cut my hand, but mostly they lacerated his face and made him back away into his pals as he put his hands to his left eye where blood was gushing onto his cheek.

I didn't pause. I stepped forward and smashed my instep into his balls, and as he doubled up, I drove a straight lead into his jaw. He fell back against his friends, obstructing their path. I reached out with my left hand and grabbed a full bottle of Jameson's whiskey. Simultaneously I kicked Red Beard hard in the chest so he collapsed at Olaf's feet, and they stumbled over him.

It was then I saw Olaf had a large hunting knife in his hand. But stepping over the prone Red Beard, he had momentarily lost his footing. I didn't swing the bottle in a wide arc this time. I used my core and drove it hard in a short stab into his temple. It stunned him long enough, while Pig's Penis with the ring in his nose pushed him from behind, to smash the bottle on the counter and drive the jagged edge of shattered glass into his throat and slash savagely sideways. He went down bubbling.

Pig's Penis and his last remaining pal backed up. I stamped on Red Beard's neck as I went by and lunged forward to drive the shattered bottle which I still had in my hand into Pig's Penis' large gut. The pain made him scream, and as he moved his hands to protect his belly, I grabbed his long hair and dragged his head to the side to slam the jagged edge of the Jameson's bottle into his jugular at the side of his neck.

I was aware the kitchen door had opened, but I ignored it. I had one Angel left, and I did not want to kill him.

For the first time, I saw him in detail. He had a death's head tattooed on his forehead, two long braids at the side of his head, and his beard was braided down to his waist. He wasn't scared. He was sneering. He had a long switch-blade, and he rushed me with it, screaming like a demented banshee.

There are lots of theories about how to defend yourself from a knife attack. Grab the wrist and twist, trap the forearm with your forearms, force his arm back over his own shoulder, grab his sleeve not his arm—in my opinion they are all bull-shit because they will all lead to your getting your hand and your wrist shredded by the blade as you try to hold on. All your assailant needs to do is move his own wrist half an inch, and he is digging deep into your hand or your forearm.

Plus anyone attacking you with a knife is going either to thrust and stab underhand or slash with the blade held back along the forearm. Both positions make trapping the arm pretty much impossible.

There is only one reliable, relatively effective way to defend yourself from a knife attack, and it was what I used on the braided death's head. I feinted forward like I was going to jab at his face but instead rammed the heel of my boot into his kneecap. Do it hard enough and fast enough, and he will go down.

This guy was tough. He went down, but he did not let go of his knife. He struggled to get into a sitting position, but I stamped hard on his knee again, and he fell back, shouting out with pain. I stepped on his wrist and spoke quietly to him.

"Let go of the knife or I will kill you."

He let go, and I kicked the blade away. Jan and Sigrid approached. They both looked sick.

I snarled at them, "Go back to the kitchen. You don't want to see this."

Jan spoke to himself. "There are four of them," he said. "My God, you are brutal."

Sigrid said, "What have you done?"

A sudden surge of anger made me snarl at her too. "What did I do? I defended myself against four men who tried to kill me! Is that ethically acceptable to you?"

I glared at Jan. "Get the hell out of here, will you! Both of you! Go back to the damned kitchen and prepare a bucket with bleach and a mop!"

They left, and I knelt down beside Death's Head.

"You've seen what I've done to your friends." He had gone waxy and was trying hard not to show the pain that must have been crippling. "So I am going to ask you again, did you work for Blue Beard at the Ravnereiret, or do you work for Dante Gallo?"

"*Faen deg!*" He growled it, and it actually meant 'fuck you.' Unfortunately, it sounded exactly like 'fun day,' which wasn't precisely what he was having.

I shook my head at him and pulled the Fairbairn and Sykes from my boot. "It's not worth it," I told him. "Be smart. Your broken knee will heal if you get to a doctor soon. But it's pointless to die protecting a secret I will find out anyway, sooner or later."

He must have seen the logic in it, and besides the pain was building, and he was looking real sick. He was waxy pale, and he had beads of sweat on his forehead.

"Blue Tooth manage the Ravnereiret, but it is belonging to Dante Gallo."

"Now see? I already knew that, and that was not what I asked you. Blue Tooth is dead, yet here you are, trying to kill me. So are you working for Dante Gallo? Did he send you?"

He hesitated, and I could see his pupils dilating as he lost focus. Then he nodded. "He pays oss..."

The kitchen door opened, and Jan and Sigrid came out. They looked mad. Sigrid had a bucket and a mop. Jan had a first aid case. I looked back at Death's Head.

"Why has he got you on this island? Is he trafficking heroin?"

His face clenched like an angry fist, and he spat on the

floor beside me. "We not touch heroin. He look for us and pay us to stop Russian bastard…"

I swore softly under my breath. I heard Jan say, "Let me get to him."

I told Death's Head, "Give me your cell."

He pulled it from his pocket. I took it, got to my feet, and walked away. After a moment's thought, I went over to where Sigrid had turned her back on the three dead men and had covered her face with her hands. I told myself there was nothing like a bit of moral ambiguity to screw up your day, grabbed Olaf's feet, and dragged him out into the freezing wind and the snow. I repeated the operation with the two other guys, and by the time I went back inside, wiping the stinging flakes from my eyes and my face, Sigrid was mopping the blood from the floor.

I sat at a table, scrolled through Olaf's address book, and found Dante Gallo. I pressed call but got the same signal Sigrid had gotten before. I went to where Jan was improvising a splint from a broken chair and asked Death's Head, "What's your name?"

"Fuck you!"

"OK, Fuck You, if you don't want me to break your other knee, how many of you are there at Gallo's place, and how do you communicate with him when the phones are out?"

Jan was staring up at me like he intended to do something about me. I gave him a fractional shake of the head.

Fuck You said, "There are twelve of us after the fire. Now you killed my friends, there are eight, and me crippled. There is radio out in the truck."

I nodded, but before I turned to leave, I told him, "You're a lucky man. You're alive because you don't traffic heroin. You should know that."

I turned and went back out into the freezing wind and the drifting snow. They had a Ford Ranger parked beside the Toyota. I trudged over to it, yanked open the door, and climbed inside. I slammed the door and shut out the howling and wailing of the gale. There was a radio beside the screen. I picked up the microphone, pressed the talk button, and said, "This is a message for Dante Gallo from Saul Goldman at Jan's bar in Asketreby. Three of the four men you sent are dead. The fourth has a broken knee. It would be very advisable for you to present yourself here as soon as possible. Over."

I let go of the button and waited for a count of five. Then the radio crackled. "Who is this?"

I thought about telling them it was a fun day but replaced the radio instead and made my way back into the bar. Death's Head was on the floor covered in a couple of blankets, and he had started shivering. Sigrid was finishing her mopping, and Jan stood to face me as I closed the door and shut out the gale.

"I want you to leave," he said.

I stopped dead and stared at him. In my peripheral vision, I could see that Sigrid had done the same.

"Really. Where do you suggest I go, Jan? It's not great weather for camping."

"I don't give a damn where you go, Saul. You get out of my bar and out of the hotel."

I gave a small sigh. "Yeah, well, you have a fun day too, Jan. Dante Gallo will be calling before long, and I plan to be here to talk to him. If that gives you a pain in the ass, I suggest you take an aspirin."

I sat at a table near the bar, and he took four strides to where I was sitting. I could see now he was carrying a Glock. Sigrid saw it at the same time I did and screamed out, "Dad! No!"

He stopped six feet from me. "I'm telling you, Saul, get out of my bar, get out of my daughter's life, I don't want any more of this in her life. Just go."

"But it's OK if you kill me from hypothermia?"

"I'm not going to argue with you. Get up and get out."

I held his eye a moment. "No."

I didn't say it with any special emphasis. But I watched his face go waxy and his pupils became pinpricks.

"I won't tell you again, Saul. Get up and get out."

"No. If you're going to shoot me, shoot me. But if you're trying to protect your daughter from more violence, this is a pretty stupid way to do it. Gallo is on his way. If you're smart, you'll take Fuck You here and leave us to it. If you insist on staying, I can't guarantee what the outcome will be. Either way, I will be gone by tomorrow. Now put your gun away and relax."

"Dad..." We both looked at her. "Please, no more. Leave him be."

He sighed heavily and sat. Outside, the gale screamed.

SEVENTEEN

IT WAS ABOUT HALF AN HOUR LATER THAT THE door opened onto the blackness outside, and an Angel the size of Godzilla came in. He held the door open, and a second man came in after him. He was maybe six foot, in a long military coat and what looked like an Australian bush hat on his head. He paused a moment to stamp the snow from his boots, then removed his hat and smoothed his hair as he took us in. He was in his seventies, but you could see it had been seventy years that had taken their toll. His eyes were the eyes of a cornered animal, and he was gaunt, almost skinny, as though life itself had ceased to nourish him.

He handed his hat to Godzilla as a third man came in. This one was tall too, in his thirties, with powerful arms and shoulders. He wore a black woolen hat and an

Australian Driza Bone coat which came down almost to his ankles. He closed the door behind him, and the three of them stood looking at us.

It was the older man who spoke.

"Jan, Sigrid, what is this? Can you explain?"

Jan stood. "Dante, we can't explain. If anybody needs to explain, it's this man here." He pointed at me. "His name is Saul Goldman."

Dante Gallo raised an eyebrow at me. "Mr. Goldman? Would you please explain to me what is going on? My club is burned down, my manager and his men are murdered"—he gestured toward the door with an open hand—"three more of my men are murdered, and I am summoned in the middle of a snowstorm. Please. Explain."

I pointed to the chair across the table from me. "Will you sit down and have a drink?"

He and the guy in the wool hat stared at me through narrowed eyes for a long count of five. Then he took a deep breath and sighed before he joined me at the table. What surprised me was that the guy in the woolen hat came and sat next to him. Gallo glanced at Jan and said, "Whisky, please, Jan. Leave the bottle. And bring coffee."

I looked at his pal. "Who are you?"

"Lieutenant John Fletcher." He pronounced it 'left-enant,' the way the Brits do.

"What regiment?"

"Mind your own damned business and answer the questions. Why are you targeting Mr. Gallo's men and property? Why have you summoned him here in the middle of this blizzard?"

"You're making a lot of demands there, Lieutenant. Are you sure you're in a position to make them?"

He leaned forward, and his eyes were like flint. "I have three dead men out there and one missing. I don't give a damn whether I'm in a position to make demands. I want an explanation."

I turned to Dante Gallo as Jan placed a bottle on the table with three shot glasses. Dante opened it and poured.

"I'm looking for someone," I said. "I think you might know where he is."

He met my gaze, and his eyes shifted and moved like he was trying to read my face. "I?" he said. "How should I know where your man is? I am a hermit on this island. I don't even go to my business in Trondheim."

He knocked back his drink, and as he set down the glass, I said, "This would be from before."

"Before...?"

"I understand you used to go by the name Adem Kodro."

He turned his eyes on Jan. There was deep resentment in them. "What I told you was in confidence. How much have you said to this man?" He didn't wait for an answer.

He turned back to me. "Who are you? Why are you here asking these questions?"

"I told you. I am looking for a man."

"You are looking for Adem Kodro?"

"No."

"Who then?"

"Did you ever go by any other name, Mr. Gallo? Before Adem Kodro, did you go by any other name?"

He had gone rigid. I had expected that. What surprised me was that the lieutenant had gone rigid too. Eventually Gallo said, "What name?"

I laughed out loud. "What, that makes a difference? If it was one name you had one, but if it's another you didn't?"

Lieutenant Fletcher snarled, "He doesn't have to tell you a damned thing."

"Yeah." I turned to him and smiled. "And you know as well as I do, Lieutenant, because you have done the interrogation training, that your answer just confirmed that he did in fact go by another name." I turned to Gallo. "Right?"

"I am asking just what name you are looking for. I am not saying yes I did nor no I did not. What name? What name you are looking for?"

I regarded him a moment, then turned back to the lieutenant. "Air Service or Boat Service?"

"What's it to you?"

I raised my shoulders an eighth of an inch. "We had standards. Makes me wonder how you wound up in an outfit like this." I turned back to Gallo. "You're not Italian. You're a Croat."

The thing about the autonomic system is that you can't consciously control it. And if you make a statement like, "You're a Croat," and the guy's face flushes red, you know he's probably Croatian. At the very least, you have touched an exposed nerve.

He looked at Jan again, and as Jan began to shake his head, I interrupted.

"Forget it. He didn't tell me. He told me you were Bosnian. It's your accent. Ninety people out of a hundred would never know. But I know the Croatian accent, and I know you're a Croat."

"So what? So I am a Croat. This is a crime?"

I frowned at him. "Who's talking about crimes, Mr. Gallo?"

He gave a humorless laugh that said he was an old hand at this kind of shit and looked at the lieutenant. It was a 'Can you believe this guy?' kind of look.

"You are killing my men, burning my property, so I am thinking about crimes. Now I ask again, so I am a Croat, so what?"

I spoke very quietly. "I am asking the questions, Mr. Gallo. I am curious about what made you call your company Sokol." I waited a moment. He stared at me with no expression. I said, "Sokol in Croat means hawk, doesn't it?"

"Again, Mr. Goldman, so what?"

"Does it mean hawk?"

"Yes."

"What made you call your shipping company Hawk, Mr. Gallo?"

His smile was more of a sneer. "I like hawks, Mr. Goldman. Is this also a crime?"

"Does the town of Sisak mean anything to you?"

He went very still. "Is a town in Croatia."

"What connection do you have with it, Mr. Gallo?"

"Nothing..." He must have weighed it up then because he shrugged and said, "I was born there."

"How about the town of Babina Planina? Does that mean anything to you, Mr. Gallo?"

His face went noticeably gray, and he swallowed. He didn't answer for a long moment. I knew what was going on in his mind. If he said it meant nothing to him, that would be as good as an admission of guilt, because every Croat of his age would know about Babina Planina. But if he admitted he knew, he risked being drawn into a discussion that could arouse dangerous emotions in him. Finally he nodded.

"Of course."

"What meaning does it have for you, Mr. Gallo?" I

paused a beat, and as he drew breath, I asked, "Were there hawks there?"

He took so long to answer that the lieutenant turned to look at him. Finally Gallo cleared his throat.

"Is near Sisak. Serbian terrorists were hiding near this village. Special police were sent to that town to find the Serbian terrorists."

"Special police from Sisak?"

"Yes." He nodded. "Elite group of anti-terrorist specialists."

"What were they called?"

He hesitated, licking his lips. "Sisak Special Operations Division."

"What was their nickname? What were they known as by the people involved?"

His response was wooden. The lieutenant was watching him closely. Gallo said, "I don't know."

"Seriously?"

"I don't remember."

I leaned forward with my elbows on the table. "I think they were called the Hawks." He didn't say anything. "Don't you think that was a bit reckless of you, Mr. Gallo...? Don't you think it was a bit arrogant? To name your shipping company after that particular special police unit?"

"It is just coincidence."

I smiled. "Now you as a cop should know coincidences very, very rarely occur." He didn't deny he was a cop, so I let it slide. "Tell me what went down at Babina Planina. How many Hawks went there?"

"I don't know."

"Forty? Fifty?"

"Maybe, I don't know."

"That's a lot of men. That would be like ten Land Rovers." He didn't answer. "What were they going to do? Go door to door, knocking, asking, 'Do you know anything about Serbian separatists...?' Is that what they were planning to do?"

"I don't know."

I waited, holding his eye. "How many people died in Babina Planina that day?"

His voice came out thick, like it was trapped in his throat.

"I don't know."

"No." I shook my head. "No, I don't believe you. I don't believe anyone from Sisak could forget something like that." I smiled at the absurdity. "You remember the name of the special police unit, but not how many people died?" I shook my head again. "No."

I sagged back in my chair. "See, the thing is, you don't need to remember, Mr. Gallo. And any Croat who had lived in Sisak would know this. Because everybody died. Everybody in Babina Planina was killed. Old men, old women, *all* the women, children, babies. Everybody was massacred." I paused, watching his face. "By the Hawks."

The only noticeable change was that his breathing had grown a little faster. He still said nothing, so I pushed him.

"Did you not remember that, Mr. Gallo?"

"Is—" He swallowed. "Is long time ago. Another life. Another world. Was..." His voice faded. "Was different."

"Different?" I picked up my glass and drained it. As I set it down, I asked him, "What was different, Mr. Gallo?"

He didn't answer. He just said, "Long time ago." He picked up his coffee, drained it, and refilled it from the pot.

"Was it that for forty years the state could do what it liked, with no accountability to anyone, and then suddenly it turned out the whole world was watching, and there were consequences?"

His face changed suddenly, twisted into a venomous mask. "Serbians were animals!"

I gave a small shrug. "A people have a right to protect themselves, but there is a limit."

He leaned forward, his face flushed, pointing at me. "Limits? Where are Serbian limits? They murder! They rape! They torture! Well, now it was their turn!"

"At the hands of the Hawks!"

His face clenched, and his voice became a hoarse rasp. "At the hands of the Hawks!"

I refilled my glass and sat looking at him. We both knew it had not been a confession.

"It must be bad," I said, "to spend the rest of your life too ashamed of who you are even to admit your name." I picked up my glass and studied it. "Too humiliated in the eyes of the world, in the eyes of normal, decent people, ever to be able to admit to the world who you are, because it's just too damned shameful."

I held his eye. His face was flushed red, and his eyes were bright with anger and pain. I pointed at the lieutenant. "He is John Fletcher." I pointed at Jan and Sigrid. "He is Jan Olafsen, and she is Sigrid Olafsen. I am Harry Bauer." I paused for a beat. "Who are you, Sergeant?"

"Shame?" He spat the word at me. I turned to Fletcher.

"Just so you know, Lieutenant. They herded up the whole town and crowded them into the main square. They wanted to know where the men were, where the militia were hiding. So they began systematically to kill the children until the mothers broke and confessed where the men were, where the militia were hiding. And once these Hawks had their information, they massacred everyone in the village, from the oldest to the youngest baby." I turned back to the old man. "Yeah," I said. "Shame. Have you got the stomach to tell us your name, Sergeant?"

He stared at the glass in front of him for a long time. "You have come here to kill me. Who sends you? Serbia?"

"I didn't come here to kill you. I came here to find out who you are."

He nodded a few times, like that made sense to him. "And did you find out who I am?" I didn't answer. He shrugged and shook his head. "It makes no difference. You have decided to kill me." He picked up his coffee and drank it, then followed it with a shot of whisky. "For men like me, it is not proof beyond a reasonable doubt. For men like me, the balance of probability is enough. 'He is Croatian, he is hiding his name, he calls his company Hawk. That is enough. He is the Butcher of Babina Planina, the sadistic sergeant from Sokol who kills women and children.' So will you kill me now? Or must I wait, looking every day over my shoulder?"

I took a handkerchief from my pocket and leaned forward to take his glass and his cup with it. "Sigrid, could you get me a plastic bag from the kitchen, please?" To Gallo, I said, "I would not kill a single person based solely on my opinion, much less an entire town. But if you are who I think you might be, and this saliva and fingerprints confirm it, then I will come for you."

All the color drained from his face. "No," he said. "There is nothing to make the comparison! There is no..." He shook his finger in the negative. "No, you are trying to trick me."

"Dr. Josip Harvat has supplied us with samples. What do you think? Do you think they will match?"

He got unsteadily to his feet. He turned and took a couple of steps. Godzilla came forward and give him his hat. He stared at it like it had lost all its meaning, then turned back to face me, like it was my fault. Lieutenant Fletcher stood. He was also watching me.

Gallo said, "Shame? Humiliation?" He came another couple of steps closer and stared down at me. "No, no shame, no humiliation. The Croat who exterminates these bastards is a proud man."

I held his eye. "Has that proud Croat the stomach to tell his name?"

He turned and walked to the door. Godzilla opened it for him, and they went out. Lieutenant Fletcher stayed a moment looking at me. All he said was, "Babina Planina?"

I nodded once. "The Sisak Hawks."

At the door, he stopped and turned back. "You were a blade?"

"Eight years."

He pushed out into the darkness, and the door closed behind him.

EIGHTEEN

"Get me two plastic bags." I said it as I pulled my cell from my pocket. Sigrid looked queasy but went to the kitchen. I dialed.

"Harry, any news?"

"Yeah, maybe—"

"You're breaking up."

"I'm in a blizzard. I have a cup and a glass with Gallo's prints and DNA. Did you get samples from Dr. Harvat?"

"You say you have prints and DNA?"

"Yes!" I raised my voice and emphasized each word. "Did Dr. Harvat get samples?"

"We're working on it."

"I need a chopper!"

"A chopper?"

"As soon as you can. For the samples!"

"You're breaking up."

"*Send a chopper for the samples!*"

His reply was all crackles. I hung up telling myself a confession from Gallo was as good as his DNA.

Sigrid emerged from the kitchen with a couple of plastic grocery bags. I took the cup and the glass and wrapped them carefully.

"A chopper will come when the storm eases. A man will come and ask for these. I am trusting you to hand them over untouched. If Gallo is not the guy, this will let him off the hook. If he is, then he deserves what's coming to him. Are we agreed?"

She nodded. I looked over at Jan, who was standing silent by the bar. He nodded. "I want it proved before you do anything to him. Beyond a reasonable doubt."

I sighed. "Believe it or not, Jan, that's what I want too. I am not a homicidal maniac out to kill anyone who strikes me as suspicious. If this guy did what I suspect he did..." I trailed off and shrugged.

"I heard what your Bogdan Novac did. He deserves whatever is coming to him."

"But if this guy is not Novac, I have no interest in him. You have to understand that. And the best way to prove it is for the cup and the glass to arrive safely at the lab."

I was far from confident, but I had little choice, and in any case, what I knew but they didn't was that we had, as yet, nothing to compare it with. I handed the bags to Sigrid and looked her in the eye.

"It would be a really stupid mistake to tamper with this. It could cause a lot of problems for a lot of people. You understand me?"

It was Jan who answered. "We understand you...Harry?"

I smiled. "Harry was a friend of mine. He died recently, but there was a chance Gallo and Fletcher might have heard of him. Let's leave it at that." I hesitated a moment. "Jan, I need to borrow your truck again."

His voice sounded dead. "What for?"

"And I need you to tell me how to get to Gallo's house."

"You're going after him, aren't you? You're going to kill him."

"No."

"I don't believe you."

"How many times do I have to tell you, Jan? That's not what I'm about. If he's Bogdan Novac, then I have a job to do. If he's not, I haven't. But now you tell me something: If he is Novac, what do you think he is going to do next? What would you do? Settle down to wait for the lab results?"

It was Sigrid who answered. "He'll start to prepare his escape."

Jan said, "You did it deliberately. You bluffed him. You

don't have any samples. You tried to put a scare into him to see how he reacts."

I didn't answer. He went on.

"If he goes back to his daily routine, you keep investigating, but if he prepares his escape, you kill him."

"It's not as black and white as that, Jan."

"You're a cold son of a bitch."

"Yeah, Jan." I nodded. "I am, and you're alive today because of it. Now are you going to lend me your truck or not?"

"No." He stared at me a moment, then started shaking his head like he was denying some internal dialogue. "I am not going to be a party to this. It's the very foundation of our civilization that we do not execute people without a trial. I will not be a party to some guy showing up out of nowhere and saying, 'I can prove this guy is a Nazi, and you have to help me murder him!' Screw you! No!"

"I am not going to kill him, Jan. All I want is to know whether—"

"No! No, so what are you going to do, kill me too because I am giving help and support to someone you believe is a war criminal? Where does it stop, Saul? And is that even your name? Where does it end? Anyone who—"

"Shut up. You don't want to lend me your truck, that's fine."

Sigrid spoke quietly. "You can take mine, but I come with you."

"That's impossible. The risk is too high."

She gave her head a single shake. "I agree with my father—" She faltered over the name. "Whoever you are. What you are doing is a crime in every civilized country in the world. But I also agree with you. If he is Bogdan Novac, he deserves to die. And if the law can't touch him, then somebody has to take the law into their own hands. So I come with you, and I make sure you stick to your word. If you don't, at least I will be a witness to it."

Jan flared up, striding toward us, gesticulating. "There are competent authorities! Report him! Call the police! Report him to The Hague. There are a hundred things you can do rather than murder him! And now you drag my daughter into your barbarism! You are as bad as you say he is. For God's sake, *think about what you are doing!*"

For a moment, he had me. For a moment he represented everything I wanted to believe in. For a moment he represented everything I wanted to believe was good and decent about human beings. But it didn't last. Too often I have seen how the naïve pursuit of ideals in a world where violence reigns leads irresistibly to the pain and suffering of the weak and the vulnerable, while the ruthless and the cruel grow strong.

I opened the door, and Sigrid stepped out without looking back at her father. I paused on the threshold. "For the last time, Jan. I am not going to kill him. I only want to know how he is reacting to the threat of the DNA tests."

He held my eye for a beat, then seemed to sag. "Let's not kid ourselves, Harry. We both know that's a lie."

I turned and left.

We trudged across the snow, now more than ankle deep, and went around behind the hotel. There she unlocked the large, wooden doors of what looked like a barn, and I helped her drag them open. Inside there was a RAM 3500. We clambered inside. She fired it up, the huge engine roared, and we pulled out into the black night, shrouded in luminous blue-white snow.

We drove in silence. Though the road was invisible, and in the blackness there seemed to be no reference points to fix our location, still she seemed to know where she was going, and the great truck seemed to skim easily over the rough terrain under the snow.

Eventually we came to the crossroads. To the left was the burned-out club. Ahead and slightly to the right, the road led to the smoldering shell of Boris' house. In my memory, there were no other options, but Sigrid spun the wheel right, and we began to crawl slowly over uneven terrain, lurching and sometimes skidding and sliding as the snow grew heavier and deeper. The island was largely flat, but I noticed that as well as apparently driving cross-country, we were climbing up a hill.

After a few minutes, the ground began to level off, and up ahead, I began to see the faint glimmer of lights.

"Kill the headlights."

She killed them, and we continued to crawl and lurch forward, toward the glimmering constellation ahead of us. Soon I could see that the lights seemed to be on three levels and, as we drew still closer, that they were behind a large stone wall with a solid gate that stood closed.

She came to within fifty yards and stopped. She spoke without looking at me. "So what's your plan? Knock on the door and ask him how it's going? Or are you going to scale an eight-foot wall in the snow?"

I ignored the smart-ass sarcastic tone and pointed to the right.

"Pull down the side of the house and back up to the wall. The flatbed is at least four feet off the ground."

She did as I said and a couple of minutes later came to a halt with the tailgate pressed up against the rock and cement wall. The snow was growing heavier, and as I swung down, I found myself knee-deep, and the big wheels of the truck were half buried in frozen sludge.

I used one of the wheels as a step and pulled myself into the flatbed. The flakes were falling fast, but so far, they were not wind-driven. Wiping the snow from my eyes, I checked the top of the wall for broken glass and found, as I had expected, that it was encrusted with broken bottles. I turned to Sigrid and found she had anticipated me and was holding out a thick blanket folded several times over. I took it, threw it over the glassy teeth, lay across it, swung my legs over, and dropped eight feet into the thick snow. As I struggled to my feet, above me I saw Sigrid's form lean over the wall and drop down beside me. I pulled her to her feet and hissed in her ear, "*What the hell are you doing?*"

"*I told you I was coming with you.*"

"*Not into the house! Are you crazy? If I am right about these people, do you realize what they can do to you?*"

She didn't raise her voice. She held my eye and spoke quietly. "I told you I was coming as a witness. I am staying."

"*They could kill you! Worse—*"

"So like a man to think that rape is worse than death."

"*I am talking about torture! And will you keep your damned voice down!*"

"Come on, your only way in is through the front door." She started to move away. I took hold of her arm, and she turned back to face me. Her tone was still quiet, but not a whisper. "The windows are too high and the walls are impossible to scale. Besides, most of them will be in the big living room with the big fire. He might have a couple on the door. We'll have to see." She went to move but stopped and looked back at me. "Besides, if you are just here to observe, why the secrecy?"

I didn't answer. I made my way at a slow wade

through the deepening snow toward the front of the house. It was massive and white, a tower of whitewashed concrete with small, narrow windows set at a height where they could not be reached without the use of a long ladder. And even if you made use of long steps, the glass gave the impression of being virtually unbreakable.

The front doors were in the same impenetrable theme. A good eight feet tall and five feet across, it was covered in some kind of beaten metal. Sigrid came up beside me.

"There is no way in. You cannot get through that door."

"I don't need to get in," I said. "I just need to get them out."

She looked at me like I was crazy. "How the hell are you going to do that?"

I pointed up at the weatherhead where the electricity cables connected with the corner of the house. "Two things you need in a snowstorm: light and heat."

I pulled my Sig from my belt, took careful aim, and blew out the housing where the cables connected with the house. At first, nothing happened. There was just the faint, luminous glow of the walls in the darkness and the drifting snow.

Maybe five minutes passed. The house must have been dark inside, and they probably needed time to find flashlights and lamps, but eventually, the big doors opened out, and two guys with flashlights emerged and played their beams along the roof, searching for the cables.

I turned to Sigrid and hissed at her, "*Go back to the truck and wait for me. These guys are dangerous, and if they find you here—*"

But she was already shaking her head. "No."

I sighed, rose from where I was lying behind a bush in the snow, and sprinted for the door. She came close behind me. Visibility was poor, and in any case, they were down the side of the house, staring up at the shattered weatherhead. They didn't see us, and we slipped through the door into the darkened hallway.

It was hard to make out much detail in the darkness, but we didn't have time to let our eyes adjust. Directly ahead, there seemed to be empty blackness and what might have been the faintly luminous form of an elevator shaft. But immediately on our left, just inside the door, was a broad staircase that seemed to ascend in a wide curve.

I sprinted silently up. As I reached the halfway mark, I began to hear the quiet murmur of voices, and on the ceiling of the landing above, I saw the wavering orange light of a fire. Then I saw the half-open door of a room from which the light was emanating.

NINETEEN

I PULLED THE SIG FROM MY WAISTBAND AND
stood very still, listening. What had been at first a murmur
of voices now resolved itself into two or three distinct
male voices speaking quietly, and just at the back of that
sound was the sound of crackling, burning wood.

I turned to Sigrid and pressed my finger against my
lips. She nodded once, and I moved silently to the landing.
Behind me, down in the well of darkness, I could hear the
two guys coming back into the house. I gestured to Sigrid,
and she slipped past me into the shadows on the landing
above. I followed, and as I flattened myself against the
wall, I heard a single pair of heavy boots stomping up the
steps. I watched his dim shape move in through the open
door, bathed in the light of the flames.

"The power cable has come away from the wall."

Gallo's voice came back, raised in anger. "How? Come away from the wall how?"

"Is hard to tell, Colonel, in this light and the snow, but it looks like it has been smashed."

Colonel.

"Smashed? How can it be smashed? There is no wind. What you have, extra powerful snowflakes in Norway? Did you see anything else—footprints, any kind of tracks, a dead bird...?"

"No, Colonel. We checked, but there was nothing unusual."

"Did you check outside? Did you check the perimeter?"

"No, sir. We assumed you want us to fix the cable..."

"It is that American. Jan has betrayed us."

And then a third voice, cracked with age, a rasp, "You are being paranoid. You are going crazy in your old age."

The colonel, whom I had recognized as Gallo, raised his voice to a yell. "I am paranoid? It is my paranoia that has you alive today!"

There was some muted, muttered response, to which Gallo responded with a tirade in a foreign language which I partly recognized as Croatian. The Norwegian who had been out in the snow interrupted the flow.

"You want us to fix the cable? Or we get by on logs and lamps?"

"Go and look! Look again!"

The old rasp cut across him. "Fix the cable. When you have light, look outside the wall for the colonel's ghosts."

The guy in the doorway turned, and as he passed to make his way down the stairs, I saw that he was one of the Angels, with long, straggly hair and a big gut. He lumbered down, shouting, "We gotta fix it. We need the ladder and the toolkit and some heavy-duty connectors."

I heard him reach the bottom and his boots tramp into the shadows, where I now realized they must have some kind of workshop, maybe even a garage. I took two long strides across the landing so I was beside the door. The voices now came clearer and louder.

"You are becoming a liability with your paranoia. So desperate to escape prison, you build a prison of your own."

Gallo's voice came back with a venomous hiss. "Perhaps I should have left you in Croatia, then!"

"Maybe it would have been better! Better than living a paranoid life in the shadows, isolated, terrified, among snow and rocks and endless night! We are multimillionaires, and we can buy *nothing!*"

"You ungrateful..."

"In case we are seen!"

"You owe me your life!"

"In case we are seen!" The voice became increasingly mocking. "In case we are seen!"

"*You would be dead without me!*"

"*In case we are seen! We are ghosts! Invisible ghosts of the undead! You will drive us all to madness on this island!*"

Gallo's voice became hysterical. "*What I am telling you, you stupid old man, is that we must leave this island! He has found us! You want to leave the island! I am telling you we must leave the island! You stupid old man!*"

I moved around the door. Gallo was standing in the middle of the floor, bathed in red and orange light. Across the room, there was a tall, narrow window through which luminous blue-white snow glowed. Beneath the window, an old man sat in a wheelchair beside a huge fireplace where large logs burned, bathing the room in heat and glowing, flickering light. Neither man saw me. They just stared hatred at each other.

"Where are you going, Colonel?" I said. "The world is shrinking, and men like you are running out of places to hide."

"So you are here."

"Did you think I'd be satisfied that easily?"

He shook his head, gazing down into the flames. "You will never be satisfied until you see me dead."

The old man by the windows had been watching us. Now he pointed a trembling hand at Gallo. "He is a cruel, sadistic man! He abducted me! He took me away from my home because he said men would come looking for us to kill us."

"Who are you?" I asked.

Gallo snarled, "Say *nothing!*"

"Who is your friend, Gallo?"

He laughed. "You still call me Gallo because you know you cannot prove I am Novac. But still you accuse me and attack me, though you have no proof."

"Who is your friend?"

"He is my uncle. He is no concern of yours! Leave him alone!"

"*Lies!*" The old man screamed it before Gallo had even finished speaking. "Lies! Lies! Lies!" He pointed a trembling hand at Gallo, half rising out of his chair. "He lies! He abducted me! I am his prisoner! He is a sadist and a killer. He keeps me in prison here!" He reached toward me with both hands, begging, "I used to have a life. I used to see friends!" He grinned broadly, remembering. "Yes! Friends. We go to dinner. We go to a concert." He gestured right and left, as though indicating the restaurant and the concert hall. "We go sailing in a yacht. And then this maniac comes, like a paranoid psychotic *fool!* 'You must come with me! You must come with me! For your own security!'"

"*Shut up!*" It was Gallo. "*You stupid old man! Shut up! You will get us all killed!*" He turned to me. "He is old and senile. He talks rubbish! You cannot make a judgment on the things a crazy old man says! It would be..." He moved toward me, holding out his hands. "It would be as immoral as the crimes you seek to punish. It would be a moral outrage to base your judgment, your capital judgment for the death sentence on the ramblings of a senile old man!"

The old man was leaning forward, half out of his chair, and I wondered if he was going to try to stand. He was pointing both feeble, scrawny arms at Gallo. "I am not senile. He is psychotic. He is a paranoid schizophrenic. Everywhere he is seeing enemies coming to hunt us down and kill us. He is psychotic. *Crazy!*"

There was a movement behind me. I didn't turn because I knew it was Sigrid. I said to her, "Do you know the man in the wheelchair?"

Before she could answer, Gallo narrowed his eyes at her. "You too, Sigrid?"

"I am here to make sure no injustice is committed, Dante."

"Is somebody going to tell me who this man is?"

Gallo snapped, "I told you he is my uncle!"

"Why does he deny it?"

"I told you this too! He is senile!"

"According to you, he's senile. According to him, you're paranoid. From where I am standing, you are not paranoid and he sure as hell is not senile. I'll tell you something else that's clear. You are both real keen to make sure nobody listens to what the other has to say." I turned to Sigrid. "You know who he is?"

"No. Sometimes, in the beginning, Mr. Gallo mentioned his uncle."

"I am not his uncle! He is liar!"

"So who are you?"

"He abduct me! He kidnap me! He take me away from—"

"I didn't ask you who he is, sir. I asked who you are."

He sat staring at me and blinking. Gallo rasped, "Stupid old man! Go on! Tell him! Tell him who you are!"

I turned to Gallo. "So who is he? I am running out of patience. Who the hell is he?"

He took another step toward me with his fingers all pinched together in a curiously Italian gesture, like he was miming the act of eating with both hands. "*He-is-my-uncle!* Will you listen to me! Maybe he is not senile, but he is stupid. He has always been stupid. Now he is old and stupid. He was enjoying his life in Croatia. When I left, I took him with me—"

"What made you do that? If he was enjoying his life back home, what made you bring him to this dump?"

He faltered for a moment but recovered. "He had acquired some enemies. It was very easy to do then in Croatia. We had all made some enemies."

"Look at me." His hands dropped by his side. He stared me in the face. "Tomorrow a helicopter will come from the mainland. It will take your cup and your glass, and it will run your DNA. If you are Sergeant Bogdan

Novac, we will know within two or three days. Tell me the truth. Why does he call you Colonel, who is he, and who are you? It's time for this to end."

The old guy in the wheelchair screamed. He sounded like a woman in a fit of hysterics, shaking his hand at Gallo, waving his finger. Gallo watched him a moment, then turned to me. "I am Bogdan Novac. After the war I was given promotions in gratitude for my services during the war. Finally I was promoted to colonel in the police." He turned and gestured at the old man. "This is my father. When I escaped from Croatia, I selfishly brought him with me as part of my cover. He had no enemies in Croatia. He was happy there. I should have left him in peace." He studied Sigrid for a moment, then looked at me. "What do you want? You want to take me outside? Should I kneel down? Stand against the wall...?"

Sigrid was staring at me. I could feel it in the semi-darkness. The firelight gave everything a feel of unreality. I said, "Shut up a minute, will you? Gallo—"

"Novac—"

Just shut up for a minute."

My mind was reeling. Everything was right. Everything was confirmed as it should be. But alarm bells were going off in my head, and I knew something was badly wrong. And suddenly the old guy was screaming again. "*I told you! I told you! I told you!*"

Gallo glared at me. "Mr. Bauer, I am telling you—"

And then the old man was pointing again, with his long, frail arm, and trembling at the end of it was a revolver. *"I warned you! If they ever come for us I will tell them! I will tell them it was you!"*

And in that moment, the lights came on. There was a fraction of a second that was timeless. I could sense Sigrid staring at Gallo. Gallo was staring at me, and his expression was one of pleading. The old man was also staring at Gallo, with the trembling pistol still clenched in his hand. But I was staring at him—at the old man in the chair. And I was staring at him because he was not old. He was no older than Gallo. He was in his late sixties, but he had been ravaged by some disease that had crippled him and withered him and reduced him to this wreck in the chair.

"He is not your father. Who is he?"

There were tears in Gallo's eyes. His voice was barely a whisper. "Please don't kill him. Look at him. God has punished him. God has taken everything from him. I am all he has, and he hates me. He lives in hell. Please, don't kill him." He came a step closer. "If you kill him, it will be a liberation for him and a punishment for me. He is the only person I have ever loved."

I pointed at the old man. "He is Bogdan Novac, and you"—I pointed at him—"are his lover."

"Yes."

It was the last thing he ever said. Because the crazy guy in the wheelchair screamed again and put three rounds through Gallo's chest. It was a fleeting moment, but as the life drained from his face, I saw the depth of his pain as he tried and failed to see across the great, black gulf that lay between him and Novac.

He took a step back, reaching for a chair, lowered himself into it and expired as the blood oozed, pulsing from the holes in his chest and the corners of his mouth.

I turned to Novac and raised my weapon, not sure if I was going to shoot him or order him to drop his revolver. As it was, I needed to do neither. Like an animated cadaver, he dropped the gun to the floor, then sat with his mouth sagging open, staring at the corpse in the chair.

"He was liar..." It was almost a whisper, like an incantation designed to give sense and meaning to that which is meaningless and grotesque.

"You are Bogdan Novac," I said.

He turned his sagging eyes and mouth on me. "Lies. You cannot prove it. You can never prove it. That..." He pointed a trembling claw. "That was Bogdan Novac. Now he is dead. They are all dead now." He leered, then laughed. "All dead now!"

"But not you, old man."

I turned. Lieutenant Fletcher was in the doorway with an Uzi in his hands.

"I never did buy the setup here. This old codger is supposed to be Mr. Gallo's dad, but you only had to see him in half-decent light and you could see they were the same age. But he kept him locked up, didn't he, where no one could see him. I couldn't make sense of it, but at first I thought it was none of my business, either. And then you started killing these bastards left, right, and center, and I began to think maybe I was involved in something deeper than just bodyguard duties." He tossed me a bag. "That's the old man's hairbrush and the glass where he keeps his false teeth. Prove he's your man, then come back for him. I'll keep him safe here for you. Come on, old codger…"

This last he said as he holstered his Uzi and took hold of the handles of the old man's wheelchair. The old man was wheezing something like a laugh as they left the room. I stood staring at Sigrid, asking myself what the hell had just happened. For a moment, his laughter seemed to become a cough. Then there was silence, followed by the loud, startling clatter of the wheelchair crashing down the stairs.

I stepped out onto the landing and found Fletcher gazing down the stairs. He turned to look at me. "Damn chair just slipped out of my grasp. Hard to tell, but I think he broke his neck." He arched an eyebrow at me. "Don't worry about it, Sergeant. If you'd heard half the conversations I have heard in this house, you'd know justice had been served."

EPILOGUE

My bags were in the Toyota, and Sigrid was at the wheel. I pushed through the door of the bar, and Jan looked up as I approached. I held out my hand to him.

"Can we part company as friends?"

He nodded and took my hand. "I owe you my life and my daughter's life. You will always have a friend in me."

We shook, and as he let go, he added, "I guess you were right all along. He had it coming. Sounds like between them they had a pretty crazy setup going on."

"Yeah, looks like Novac owned it, and as he grew more crazy, Gallo, or whatever his real name was, ran it along with Blue Tooth. You got a clean slate here now, Jan. You going to try and keep it that way?"

"You know it."

I turned to go but stopped and turned back. "One thing. It's just curiosity. You were an Angel, right?"

He leaned on the bar and gave a single nod.

"The story Sigrid remembers, about your wife and the guys you killed…"

"She half-remembers. I was recently out of the Marines. I had joined the Angels." He shrugged. "It was the freedom, after so much discipline and death… The bikes, the fuck 'em all attitude, the freedom. But it was a rival gang. They killed my wife, I killed them, and I fled."

"Blue Tooth came after you?"

"Yeah, Gallo negotiated a peace settlement, and while he was at it acquired a small army who were stashing away a lot of money for their retirement."

I nodded and left the bar. We drove in silence the short distance to the ferry, among the snowy, frozen landscapes under an ice blue sky. At the makeshift gangway, she clung to me and gave me a long, lingering kiss.

"Come back," she told me.

I had intended to say I might, one day, or we'd see how things played out, or simply perhaps. Instead I said, "I will."

And wondered why.

On the long crossing over the black water, I thought that death was neither black nor white. Death, like life, was whatever color you make it.

Don't miss THE REAPER OF ZION. The riveting sequel in the Harry Bauer Thriller series.

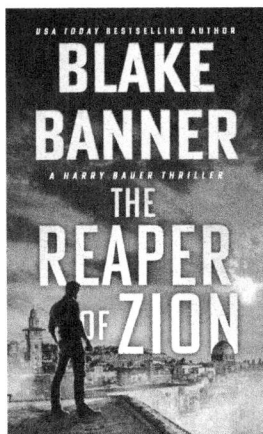

Scan the QR code below to purchase TIME TO DIE.
Or go to: righthouse.com/the-reaper-of-zion

DON'T MISS ANYTHING!

If you want to stay up to date on all new releases in this series, with this author, or with any of our new deals, you can do so by joining our newsletters below.

In addition, you will immediately gain access to our entire *Right House VIP Library,* which includes many riveting Mystery and Thriller novels for your enjoyment!

righthouse.com/email

(Easy to unsubscribe. No spam. Ever.)

ALSO BY BLAKE BANNER

Up to date books can be found at:
www.righthouse.com/blake-banner

ROGUE THRILLERS
Gates of Hell (Book 1)
Hell's Fury (Book 2)
Ice Burn (Book 3)

ALEX MASON THRILLERS
Odin (Book 1)
Ice Cold Spy (Book 2)
Mason's Law (Book 3)
Assets and Liabilities (Book 4)
Russian Roulette (Book 5)
Executive Order (Book 6)
Dead Man Talking (Book 7)
All The King's Men (Book 8)
Flashpoint (Book 9)
Brotherhood of the Goat (Book 10)
Dead Hot (Book 11)
Blood on Megiddo (Book 12)
Son of Hell (Book 13)
Merchant of Death (Book 14)

Extinction C-14 (Book 15)

HARRY BAUER THRILLER SERIES
Dead of Night (Book 1)
Dying Breath (Book 2)
The Einstaat Brief (Book 3)
Quantum Kill (Book 4)
Immortal Hate (Book 5)
The Silent Blade (Book 6)
LA: Wild Justice (Book 7)
Breath of Hell (Book 8)
Invisible Evil (Book 9)
The Shadow of Ukupacha (Book 10)
Sweet Razor Cut (Book 11)
Blood of the Innocent (Book 12)
Blood on Balthazar (Book 13)
Simple Kill (Book 14)
Riding The Devil (Book 15)
The Unavenged (Book 16)
The Devil's Vengeance (Book 17)
Bloody Retribution (Book 18)
Rogue Kill (Book 19)
Blood for Blood (Book 20)
The Cell (Book 21)
Time to Die (Book 22)
The Reaper of Zion (Book 23)

ABOUT US

Right House is an independent publisher created by authors for readers. We specialize in Action, Thriller, Mystery, and Crime novels.

If you enjoyed this novel, then there is a good chance you will like what else we have to offer! Please stay up to date by using any of the links below.

Join our mailing lists to stay up to date -->
righthouse.com/email
Visit our website --> righthouse.com
Contact us --> contact@righthouse.com

facebook.com/righthousebooks
x.com/righthousebooks
instagram.com/righthousebooks

Printed in Dunstable, United Kingdom

68537905R00139